MW01093411

THE FOREVER HOME

SALLY ROYER-DERR

Copyright © Sally Royer-Derr, 2024

The moral right of the author has been asserted.

To request permissions, contact the publisher at rights@stormpublishing.co

Ebook ISBN: 978-1-80508-404-4
Paperback ISBN: 978-1-80508-405-1

Cover design: Sara Simpson
Cover images: Shutterstock

Published by Storm Publishing.
For further information, visit:
www.stormpublishing.co

ALSO BY SALLY ROYER-DERR

The Secrets Next Door

Ohana

The Tracks

High Bluffs Trilogy

High Bluffs

Santa Monica

The Return

For Sue, my sister, my friend

ONE

2023

Aimee

I brushed back a lock of my golden hair, highlighted naturally by hours spent in the sun, and adjusted my sunglasses. I stole a glance at my husband, Archie, sitting in the driver's seat of our newly purchased SUV, black with leather interior. His golden hair was slightly darker than mine; he wasn't the outdoorsy type like me. Sure, maybe a hike here or there, but I was a daughter of nature. I crave the sunshine, fresh air and want to be part of all that is alive around me. Allow me to place my fingers into the life-sustaining earth and feel the burn of heat in the blue sky on my body, and life would spring from me.

Archie turned and flashed a smile at me. A trickle of sunshine traveled from his left temple across his sunglasses down to his mouth of perfectly straight white teeth. Not only did we share golden hair, but, in my mind, we were a golden couple. I'd been waiting to find my partner for a long time. Life threw me some curves, but when he entered my orbit everything looked brighter.

Kismet stepped in on the day we met. Me, toiling away at

my barista job, still living with my aged aunt in her Philly town-house on Society Hill, and Archie coming in to pick up a large coffee order for a local elementary school where he was a third-grade teacher.

The chemistry was undeniable. Something I hadn't felt in years. When you click with someone, feel that strong connec-tion, it's something you've always craved but wondered if you would ever find it. That's how it was between us. We married quickly soon after my aunt passed away leaving me a sizable inheritance.

"What are you thinking about?" Archie asked now, his voice breaking into my thoughts, still smiling.

I touched his hand lying on the console. "You. When we first met. I can't believe we've been married a year already."

He nodded. "I know, it went so fast."

"And now we're really doing this. This move is going to be such an adventure for us."

"Yeah, we'll be there soon."

I took a contented sigh and looked out the window at the passing scenery. Cornfields with neat, small green stalks lined the right of the road, hopefully knee-high by the Fourth of July, as I heard some locals say when we stopped by town last week, and grasses of alfalfa, still in their infancy, lined the left, a few strands blowing in the warm early summer breeze. White, puffy, cotton candy clouds hung high in the clear blue sky, their vastness seemingly endless.

Even though the air conditioning blasted inside the vehicle, I hit the automatic button and the passenger car window rolled down. Sweet-smelling summer air entered the SUV. Honey-suckle, I guessed. I'd noticed it growing along the road as we drove along. Ahead in the distance, a large blue and white sign was visible. Bright orange and yellow marigolds surrounded its base.

WELCOME TO POPLIN, PENNSYLVANIA

"We're here," I said to Archie. Finally, starting our adventure and moving into the small farm I'd salivated over since spotting it on one of the many real estate websites I'd browsed in the evenings in my aunt's townhouse. I wasn't a city girl. I wanted to be among the trees, plants, and birds. I wanted to look out my window and see endless farmland spread out like a beautiful painting, but it would be my painting, our painting. A few months ago, I found the jewel that we would call our first real home as a married couple. Sure, we lived in Aunt Lou's townhouse together, but this house was the first home we purchased together, making it so special to me, to us. A stunning, gothic-style farmhouse that sat on forty acres of land. My dream. Our dream.

"Exciting, isn't it?" Archie continued to drive, passing a few homes and the elementary school where he would teach third grade, starting at the end of August. A little farther down the road, we entered Main Street, with its picturesque stores and restaurants, many boasting bright gingerbread trim in blue, pink, and yellow. Tall, white globed streetlights lined the street among large planters filled with bursts of flowers in an array of summer blooms.

I paid particular attention to the couple of stores with a *For Rent* sign in their polished windows. Angela, the realtor who sold us the property, had mentioned a few spots were available when I told her about wanting to open a small, organic market in town. I planned to sell produce I would grow on the farm and from neighboring farms, once we were fully moved and settled in. I never realized how many details needed to be taken care of when you purchased a property. Luckily, Aunt Lou's inheritance gave us a nice cushion to do things at our own pace.

One location stood out to me every time I drove through town.

Nestled between a thrift boutique and hardware store, a small, white storefront with bright yellow trim and two large windows. An equally bright yellow double door provided entry. An ivy wreath adorned each door. It was perfect, and though it was faster than I'd meant to move, I made a mental note to mention it to Angela when we met her at the house. I wanted that store, and even though I had about a month of work to get the house ready first, I couldn't bear for anyone else to snatch up the property. I could already imagine my fresh vegetables, homemade jams and fresh-baked goods lining the shelves. And eggs. I planned to have many chickens, so was sure I'd have a good egg supply to sell to my customers.

The charming downtown was left behind us as we turned right just outside of town. Only a few minutes away, Archie pulled the vehicle onto the paved lane of our new home. I took a deep breath, the same thing I'd done the first time we toured the small farm. I'd always imagined myself living in the country, among cornfields and lonely country roads. The space and the quiet of the environment appealed to me in so many ways. Nobody too close to bother us. Only Archie and me, really all I needed in my life. This beauty was the home of my dreams. Neatly clipped grass stretched out on either side of the quarter-mile lane. Two tall oak trees struck a stately presence on each side of the lane. Dark mulch encircled the trunks, bright red geraniums sprang from the mounds. As we neared the house, I absorbed its beauty again. A two-story classic, gothic-style white farmhouse. Large, wraparound porch, freshly painted, Victorian-style turret to the rear right of the house. White gingerbread trim throughout and, my personal favorite, at the highest peak of the house, in the attic, triple stained-glass windows. The house was well maintained, but some updates were needed, although nothing that would have deterred us from making an offer on it though. I was in love the moment I saw the property. Almost as if it was waiting for me. I could still hear its whisper to me.

The lane curved to the left and ended at a detached three-car garage, also white and gingerbread trimmed. Two large terracotta planters sat on either side of the garage, bursting with dark purple petunias and white impatiens. A small, gray sedan sat parked next to the flowerpot on the left.

"That's not Angela's car," Archie remarked, putting the SUV into park.

"No," I replied. "I wonder who it is."

As I spoke, a short, balding man emerged from the house, our house. He wore a rumpled white dress shirt, dress pants, and a loosened polka dot tie. He appeared anxious.

"You must be the Greencastles." He gave us a smile. "I'm Ned from Poplin Realty. I'm here to give you your extra set of keys and see if you have any questions."

"Oh, hi, Ned." Archie opened the car door and stepped onto the driveway. He shook the man's outstretched hand.

I waved. "Nice to meet you."

"I'm confused," Archie said, "I thought Angela was meeting us today?"

Ned fumbled with his already loose tie. His face reddened and he sighed. He seemed on the verge of tears. "She would have been here, but Angela was murdered two days ago."

TWO
2023

Aimee

"Murdered!" I gasped, moving closer to Archie. He put his arm around me. "How?"

Ned sighed, clearly trying to keep his emotions in check. "She was shot, um, at a house she was showing, right outside of town."

"Wow, that's crazy," said Archie; surprise colored his voice and his eyes widened. "Any leads on who did it?"

"No, the police have tried tracing the phone call of the person requesting the showing, but the call came from an untraceable phone, so no luck. The name in her calendar was just Mrs. Smith."

"This is such sad news," I said sympathetically. "Why would someone want to kill Angela?"

Ned shrugged. "I can't imagine. She was a beautiful person, inside and out. And she was a great realtor. She sold most of the homes in this area. I'm more like her helper, or was, I guess."

I nodded, remembering seeing Angela just three weeks before when Archie and I had our final walk-through in the house. She was an attractive woman with strawberry blond hair cut in a sleek bob who dressed more upscale than the rural farm town she represented. She was always friendly and ready to answer any question we had about the property. A very sad story, indeed. I would have liked to have gotten to know her better. For a second I wondered about the safety of our new town, but it sounded like someone had targeted her specifically, from what Ned mentioned about the house showing.

"Well." Ned shrugged again. "I don't want to talk about this anymore. It's too upsetting. And it's such an exciting day for you both."

"Oh, of course," I said. "We understand. Our deepest condolences. Angela was a lovely person. Thank you for coming out to give us the keys."

We had settled on the house a few weeks earlier, but wanted to have some remodeling work completed before moving in. Archie and I would come out periodically to check on the ongoing work in the house, but sometimes we couldn't make it during the times the crew worked. Angela kept the extra keys to allow the remodeling crew and the furniture delivery people into our house. I appreciated her offering to do this for us. She really was an excellent real estate agent.

"Certainly, if you have any questions, please call me." Ned handed me his business card.

"Thank you, Ned," Archie said.

We waved goodbye as he drove his car down the lane.

We turned to face the farmhouse. Our house. It's all we'd talked about for the last few months and now, finally, it was a reality. A dream come true, I almost wanted to pinch myself to be sure it was really happening. Our first real home as a married couple. We stayed at Aunt Lou's house until it was sold, but this was our home, not someone else's we occupied.

"So," Archie said, taking my hand, "let's go into our new house."

"Hey, you're forgetting something," I reminded him with a grin.

Archie laughed and picked me up effortlessly in his arms. He walked the three steps up to the porch, flung open the white screen door, and inserted the key into the door. Gripping tightly, he carried me over the threshold and placed me on the dark walnut hardwood floor in the entryway. "Welcome home, Mrs. Greencastle," he whispered into my ear.

I twirled around, enjoying the freshly painted walls in a creamy, pale yellow and the bouquet of fresh flowers, sent from the realtor's office, that sat on the antique side table by the cushioned bench.

I was so happy our furniture had arrived before us. I had left specific instructions as to where I wanted everything placed in the house, and hoped all the pieces had been put into those designated spots. We didn't have a lot of furniture at this point; the new pieces I'd ordered online would arrive this week. I could not wait to decorate our new space.

"Come on, let's explore." I grabbed Archie's hand, and we walked back through the hall into the kitchen. My new kitchen cabinets, in mint green, were installed along with new appliances, a double oven for all my culinary experiments, dishwasher, retro bottom freezer refrigerator, also in mint green. White subway-style backsplash, white farmhouse sink, and a large butcher block kitchen island. I needed to get my small kitchen table for the breakfast nook and the room would be complete. And maybe a cushioned bench by the window.

"Wow, this looks great," Archie commented. He dropped my hand and opened the cabinets and the refrigerator. A fruit basket and six bottled waters were inside, again compliments of the realtor agency. So thoughtful.

"I think we have to go grocery shopping though," he remarked. His warm brown eyes shined. "Really, Aimee, this looks great. That contractor you hired knew what he was doing." Archie hadn't been to the property for over a week, and this was his first time seeing the kitchen renovation. I'd been here several times over the past week overseeing everything.

"Yes, he did," I agreed, running my hand over the island. I arranged everything. I had specifics in mind, and it was easier for me to make the contacts. If I really cared about something, I wanted it exactly to my specifications. Archie didn't seem to mind. He rather liked it when I took charge of things.

We checked out the dining room, still empty of furniture at this point, as well as the living room, but that furniture would arrive soon, along with a TV, mostly for Archie—I don't watch much TV, but it was nice to have for the rare occasion.

"Let's go up to the bedroom." I raised my eyebrows. "See if they set up our bed correctly." I started up the stairs.

Archie came up behind me, squeezing my bottom. "Oh, I hope so, or we'll be christening the floor."

"It won't be the first time." I laughed as he chased me up the stairs.

THREE

2023

Aimee

I uncapped a water bottle and took a long drink, admiring our new kitchen. While I wanted to preserve—and appreciated—the elegant beauty of the 1920s Victorian farmhouse, I needed a modern kitchen, while giving a nod to an old-fashioned style. The old kitchen, a remodel from the late seventies or early eighties, had cried out for an upgrade, not my style in any way. Everything else in the house only required a fresh coat of paint and refinishing the hardwood floors, to bring them back to a beautiful luster.

Archie went to get groceries alone. I wanted some time to soak in our house, feel its heart and warmth, the connection I experienced the first time Angela unlocked the front door for us. I knew this was my house, our house, straightaway. I'm intuitive to such feelings, vibrations, if you will. I'd been manifesting this house, this life, for years now, and finally, I received what I'd been visualizing for so long. We belonged here.

I walked across the kitchen and opened the back door onto a large concrete patio with a kidney-shaped pool, installed by the previous owner. The pool, covered in black winter tarp, was one of the first projects Archie and I would work on. In a week or two I hoped to be lying on a lounge chair, sipping a cold drink before taking a dip, hopefully a skinny dip, with Archie. The open farmland stretched out seemingly endless around the backyard. Beyond the white vinyl fence surrounding the pool and patio area was a sizable yard. In the back of the yard there was a large garden space, about half an acre, and I planned to expand its size; we had the space. After the garden the expansive sky spread out majestically and allowed a stunning view of the Blue Mountain range in the distance. Fields, planted with corn, small green stalks at this stage, surrounded the house, open fields all one could see. Our land. I felt like a pioneer in a sense. Land of the Greencastles.

I took a deep breath of fresh air, allowing it to fill my body with its purity. This place lived in my dreams for so long. A manifest I focused on and, finally, felt the fruits of that focus. Meditation and manifestation continued to be cornerstones in my daily journey, concepts I learned so long ago, in what seemed then like another lifetime. I took another deep breath and embraced the peace surrounding me.

All the plans I held for this place ran through my mind. Creating a new life with Archie was all I'd wanted since the day he walked into my life. He was the love of my life. Whatever I thought was love in the past certainly inferior to my experience with Archie. Funny how love finds you when you're not looking for it. Almost everything that's meant for you finds you when the time is right. Why do we spend so much time chasing things when the universe knows what we need? Mother Earth will provide for her children. All in good time.

Archie placed the last of the groceries into the refrigerator, a gallon of milk and half gallon of orange juice, and turned his attention to me, already eating the grilled chicken salad he brought me for lunch, at the kitchen island.

"Well, that's done." He grabbed his salad, took off the lid, and started eating.

"This salad is really good," I remarked. "You got it in town?"

"Yeah, right on Main, down from the thrift store," Archie said, taking a bite of salad.

"Good to know," I replied.

"And I think your idea for a market in town is great. The nearest grocery store is twenty minutes away. People will love having a closer option."

"Oh, good. I'm not going to have tons of inventory like a grocery store, but nice for fresh foods."

Archie nodded, eating his salad. "Crazy what happened to Angela though."

"Sure is," I replied. "I hope they find who did it. It's creepy thinking about a killer lurking around here."

"Yeah, it's not a place you'd think of a murder happening."

"Maybe it was a jealous husband, or boyfriend?"

"Maybe. If it is, the police should catch him soon. And we'd better keep the doors locked at all times, in case there's some psycho running around town."

I sighed. "I see your point, but that's one of the reasons we moved here, not to be worried about locking our doors."

Archie grabbed my hand. "I know, but, please, just until they catch this guy. I don't want anything to happen to my beautiful wife."

I laughed. "Wife, it still sounds funny to me even though we've been married for a year, but I love it."

"I think it sounds perfect," he replied. He took a drink of water. "So, Mrs. Greencastle, what's first on the list?"

"Pool," I said, winking at him.

FOUR
2016

The Commune
Dream

Chanting at sunrise was my favorite time at the Listening Lark commune. Orange and yellow glimpses of sky peeked through the cottonwoods and orange trees on the property. The family moved together in perfect harmony as River played his guitar and Branch pounded on the bongo drum. Peace and serenity filled my body, every one of my senses heightened, and the pure joy I felt afterward was one of my life's most rewarding experiences in my twenty-five years on this Earth.

Today she was beside me, gazing at me with her big, beautiful blue eyes. Those eyes were the first thing I noticed about her; they enchanted me right from the start. We chanted together, absorbing the energy of Mother Earth and the sun as it appeared, warming our barely clothed bodies. I wore my white cotton shorts, as I did most days, and she, her thin, long white cotton dress, with nothing underneath. Later, when we worked in the garden she'd put on her denim overalls over a bikini, then discard the overalls after work was complete, and we'd go for a soak in the hot tub located on the back patio.

It had only been about six months since I'd met this beauty at a farmers' market where we sold organic produce and hand-made jewelry for the family of Listening Lark. She'd approached our booth, admiring our wares and I admiring hers. Her hair hung long and golden, kissed by the sun, her petite frame tanned and brightened by a shining turquoise necklace she bought, made by Moonbeam, a talented crafter in our family.

Lightning sparked between us and, a month later, she dropped out of UCLA, and joined me on the commune, soaking up the southern Californian sun, together in harmony. The connection between this woman and myself fueled not only on sensual desires, but also an intimate connection I'm not sure I could even describe. I felt as if I'd been waiting my entire life to meet her. My soulmate. My goddess.

Sunshine Lotus was her new name. Brother Jim gave it to her when she joined us, as he did with all the new members. We usually called her Sunny. Her given name, Aimee, was left in the past.

We only lived in the here and now.

FIVE

2023

Aimee

I slipped on my oven mitt and opened the oven door, pulling out two muffin baking pans filled with freshly baked banana nut muffins. I inhaled the delicious aroma and placed them on the stove top next to two pans of strawberry muffins. I turned the stove off and threw my oven mitt on the counter.

My cup of tea sat on the newly purchased kitchen table, an antique white, round pedestal beauty, and I snapped it up to take a sip. The past couple weeks had been busy and the days had flown by. All our new furniture had now arrived, and we'd got everything arranged as we wanted it. Plus, Archie and I opened the pool and planted the garden, extending it a little to add a larger crop of sweetcorn to the plantings of green beans, tomatoes, peppers, peas, potatoes, onions, and cucumbers. A large strawberry patch sat at the back of the garden, and we'd been enjoying the harvest of my favorite fruit. A few blueberry bushes lay to the right of the strawberry patch. To the left of the garden space was a small orchard, about ten trees, bursting with small apples. We would plant more fruit trees soon and some more blueberry bushes.

Archie was at the elementary school today, finishing some employment paperwork in the afternoon. He seemed excited to start at a new school. He'd only been at his old school for two years, so he hadn't made any long-term connections there. We had an appointment with Ned later, at five, to see the store for rent in town. We'd go out to dinner afterward, somewhere in Poplin; I wanted to explore the town a bit more.

I sat down at our new kitchen table, still nursing my tea. I'd been thinking a lot about Angela's murder this week. No news of an arrest, at least that we'd heard, but there had been plenty of talk in the store when I'd last gone for groceries. Angela wasn't married or in a current serious relationship, which took care of the theory of a jealous lover. Archie too seemed hung up on it. He kept asking the same questions: Who would want her dead? Was it a random killing, and could the killer still be close?

A knock on the front door broke into my thoughts. I rose to answer it, pausing to look out the peephole. A young woman, a few years younger than I, stood on the other side, a friendly smile on her face. I doubted she was a murderer, so I opened the door.

She had long, straight chestnut hair and warm brown eyes, directed at me. She wore jean shorts, a blue T-shirt that read *Poplin Elementary School*, and bright white sneakers with a blue and white pom-pom on each shoe. She held a plate of chocolate chip cookies.

"Hi," she said warmly. "I'm Robin Kent. I wanted to welcome you to the neighborhood."

"Hi, Robin," I replied, accepting the plate of cookies she handed me. "I'm Aimee. Thank you."

"Of course," Robin said in a sing-song voice. "I'm your neighbor, just a five-minute drive down the road, on the right, or a ten-minute walk."

"Great to meet you," I said, smiling at the woman. She must have noticed me sneaking a glance at the pom-poms on her sneakers. She laughed.

"Oh, these." She wiggled her foot. "I coach cheerleading at the high school. I'm doing the summer program and I had a session this afternoon."

I laughed. "Well, that explains it." I pointed to her T-shirt. "Do you coach elementary students?"

"No, high school cheerleading. I teach third grade at Poplin Elementary," she said. "I'll be your husband's partner teacher. I'm his mentor, just to help him get a hang of the new school."

"Oh, how nice." I paused, mulling over the information. Well, that explained the sing-song voice, typical of many elementary teachers. But this, what, twenty-one, twenty-two-year-old would be mentoring my husband who'd been teaching for eight years? "I'm sure Archie will appreciate your help."

"It's only my second year of teaching, so he'll probably be teaching me so much!" she said enthusiastically.

Wow, she does not know when to stop. I gave her a tight smile. "I'm sure he will."

"I met Archie today at school actually," Robin continued. "So, I was excited to meet you too. You're all he talked about. Your home is so beautiful. I always loved this property."

"Thanks, Robin," I replied. Maybe she was just an overly friendly person. I'd give her the benefit of the doubt. "And it is so kind of you to welcome us. Would you like to come in for a cup of tea, or something else?"

"Sure!" Robin exclaimed, walking into the house. "Ooh, it smells amazing in here."

"I baked some muffins."

We walked into the kitchen and Robin stopped talking, for a moment.

"Aimee, your kitchen is gorgeous, wow. I'm stunned by it. I love the color, everything, really."

"Thanks," I said. "I love the color too."

I poured her a cup of tea and put two muffins on a plate, along with her cookies, and we sat down at the kitchen table. A memory flashed in my mind. How at one point, years ago, I cut all sugar out of my diet, unless it was natural sugar from fruits. That decision was one of the better ones at that point in my life that I probably should have kept up. Sugar wasn't good for the body, but it tasted so good.

She took a bite of the strawberry muffin. "So good. One day I hope to get married and have my own house. All in good time though."

"Oh, who do you live with now?" I asked.

"My parents."

"Makes sense. You're what, like twenty-two?"

"Twenty-four. Did you live with your parents at twenty-four?"

"No, I lived with my aunt. My parents died when I was seventeen."

"Oh, I'm so sorry. Car accident?"

"Yeah."

"It's great that you had your aunt then. I hope she's doing well," Robin said sympathetically.

"She passed about a year ago," I replied, taking a bite of cookie.

"Oh, sorry. I'm asking too many questions. I do that sometimes, maybe all the time." Robin laughed. "I think you'll like our town. Everyone is very friendly here and it's quiet. Well, usually."

"Have you heard anything about Angela, the realtor's murder?"

Robin shook her head. "No, that is so shocking. I can't remember the last time we had a murder around here. I grew up here and the only murder I recall was about ten years ago. It was a drug deal gone bad, that type of thing. A guy that hadn't lived here very long was shot. But Angela's murder is so different. She's been a part of our community for years. I can't believe it. She was such a kind woman. Very friendly and warm."

"She was. We only met a few times, but I spoke to her several times on the phone. Such a sad story and scary until they catch who did it."

"Very scary," Robin agreed, taking another bite of muffin.

I stared at her. She was twenty-four, but looked like she could be on the high school cheerleading team she coached. She talked a lot and was a bit too friendly for me, but despite myself, I liked her.

SIX

2016

The Commune
Dream

Sunny took a slab of butter and spread it on the homemade bread, still warm from the oven. She and I had dinner duty this evening and she was craving bread, so we made several loaves. She held the bread out to me, and I took a bite, then she did. I wiped a bit of butter that dripped down the side of her mouth.

"Dream," she said. That was my name now. I'd always been a dreamer, so it was the perfect name for me. Brother Jim knew this; he was also my cousin.

"Yes, Sunny." I loved to say her name. The syllables just rolled like honey off my tongue.

"I love you," she said, smiling. Her blue eyes gazed into mine with adoration.

"I love you too," I told her.

She turned away and poured fresh pineapple juice into her glass.

Sunday evening meant family dinner and while we practiced a mostly vegetarian diet, on Sundays we had chicken or fish, always a treat. Tonight was grilled chicken, Sunny's favorite, with green beans, carrots, romaine lettuce, and home-made bread. All the food grown by the family.

Brother Jim had given a short talk and prayer before the meal. Now everyone sat at long, simple wooden tables in the main hall of the old Spanish-style home we inhabited. It had been Brother Jim's, and my, grandmother's house which we inherited a few years ago. At one time the foyer, dining room and kitchen were all separate rooms, but several months ago we tore them down, keeping the load-bearing walls, and created a large cooking and eating space for our growing community, now numbering forty people.

Listening Lark was a utopia group, an intended community. Nothing was forced on any individual; it was your choice. Everyone was here out of choice and could leave at any time. Some rules applied, or rather guidelines. Attending chanting and meditation activities regularly and Brother Jim's talks—he preferred this term to sermons—and putting in work or mone-tary effort to fuel our good works. While money, or lack of it, did not determine if you could join the group, Listening Lark had many notable members, a couple of well-known actresses, a successful tech guru, among others who happily supported the family of Listening Lark. The family grew day by day.

We were a sexually free commune, not limited to one part-ner. Nudity was accepted here without any judgment, male or female. Many female members chose to go topless most of the time, feeling more comfortable in this state; others preferred to wear a top. Some people were nude most of the time. These were all personal choices made by the individual and not judged by other members.

Sunny was different though. Before she joined our family, I told Brother Jim, or Jim Bob, as we used to call him when he was younger, that she was off limits for any other sexual part-ners. She was only mine. He agreed; he had to, I owned half of the commune's assets, though I allowed him to be top dog. He thrived on the status. He was always an attention hog and wanted to oversee everything. Most family members didn't even know we were related. He liked the power, and I didn't care about having power, I only wanted to do what I wanted. And I wanted to be with Sunny.

I felt a bit bad that she had dropped out of college to join us. She said she didn't care. She'd been studying Psychology, maybe to eventually be a child psychologist, but she didn't care for school. She didn't want to go back to Philadelphia either, to live with her aunt; and her parents were both dead. She said she was so lonely until the day she met me and her whole world opened. I knew exactly what she meant. That day at the farmers' market was as if the universe brought her directly to me. The moment I looked into her eyes, I knew I would be with this woman until the end of time. Our meeting was not fate, it was destiny. And when the universe spoke to me, I always listened.

She said my name was perfect for me because I had walked into her life like a dream. I was Dream.

I was her dream come true.

SEVEN
2023

Aimee

Archie and I examined the small store available for rent. The hardwood floors, shining as if they'd recently been buffed, a few clothes racks sat in the center of the store. The walls were painted a pale taupe. A cash register and checkout area in the rear of the room. The back room held a small storage area, a minuscule bathroom, and a door to the rear parking lot.

"Did this used to be a clothing store?" I asked, noting the racks.

"It was the thrift store," Ned said. "They moved next door last month. They needed more space; their business really took off the last few years."

I nodded. "I would need a refrigerated case for eggs and other items. Would that be a problem to put in?"

"I'll talk to the owner," said Ned. "I don't think that will be an issue."

"Hmm... I do like this space." I looked over at Archie, who was counting the outlets. "What do you think?"

"Up to you, babe," he said. "I think it's perfect for what you want to set up though. The space is good, the location is great."

"I know, yeah." I was brimming with excitement as I turned back to Ned. "We'll take it as long as I can get a refrigerated case."

"Okay, I'll let the owner know and get back to you," Ned said.

We thanked Ned and left the empty store. I squeezed Archie's arm. "I'm so excited. Let's go celebrate!"

"I already found the perfect place," he replied as we walked to our car. "I saw it when I was coming home today. It's right past the school. Robin was talking about it the other day."

"Let's go!"

We drove the short distance, and just before the school, turned on a paved lane with a large sign at the end that read *Poplin Chicken*. The lane led into a wooded area and then turned into a sizable parking lot. There was a large red and white building emblazoned with *Poplin Chicken* on the side, and an enormous red and white chicken statue stood at the front door. The building extended to a large, enclosed patio overlooking a miniature golf course with many tiny lakes and tiny bridges going across them.

I looked at Archie and laughed. "What is this place?"

"Best barbeque chicken in Poplin, so I've been told," he said. "Let's go try some."

I smiled and we exited the car, holding hands as we paused at the enormous chicken statue, at least ten feet tall, and went inside. They had a takeout window, an ice cream window, and an entrance to the restaurant. Good to remember if we ever wanted some ice cream sundaes or quick takeout chicken. The restaurant was cafeteria style, a bit odd, but after sitting down and digging into our chicken and potato filling, and carrots, I had to admit their chicken was fantastic. So good.

"Do you love it?" Archie asked, wiping his greasy chicken lips. "Robin was right about this place."

"Totally," I said, surveying the restaurant. "This place is busy. I wonder who supplies their vegetables."

"Maybe you could?"

"Maybe next year, I don't think I'd have the quantity for this place though."

"Something to check out," Archie said. "I think I'm going to enjoy this new school."

I smiled. "I'm so glad. I want to come in and help you set up your classroom when it's time."

"Yes, I'd love that, but we don't have to think about that for another month and a half," he replied.

"Robin came by today. She brought us cookies," I remarked.

"She said she was going to visit. I like her too. I think she'll be fun to work with. She has a lot of energy."

"She sure does... and she's your mentor?" I raised my eyebrows.

He laughed. "Does that bother you?"

I put my hand on his. "Not really. I just like to tease you."

"It's good I like being teased by you," he replied with a grin that melted my insides.

"I'm glad we're getting settled here. Even with the shock of Angela's murder, I think this is the right place for us. The right place to start our life together."

"Me too," Archie agreed.

I savored this moment, sitting in a strange chicken restaurant in the middle of nowhere. There was a time when I didn't think I had any type of future ahead of me. Always running from the past. Now I was Mrs. Archie Greencastle. I was safe and whole. Archie and I were lost souls before we found one another. Neither of us had any family, and few friends. My parents died when I was seventeen; I had Aunt Lou after they passed, but she was gone now too. Archie's family was his mother and sister, and they'd died in a car accident, a few years before we met. We married at the courthouse, just the two of us. Us against the world. I rather liked it that way. Sometimes we give our trust, our friendship, our love to people that didn't deserve it, or used it. I wouldn't make that mistake again.

I learned from my mistakes.

EIGHT
2023

Aimee

The summer moved quickly, and we were into July before I knew it. I was so busy setting up the store, with Archie's help, weeding and watering the garden. The plants took off in the rich soil much to my delight. Red, plump tomatoes hung heavy on the fuzzy, thick green vines. Plants sprouted, growing green beans, sugar peas, tall green stalks bursting with Silver Queen sweetcorn. And my blossoming friendship with Robin grew, as well.

I liked Robin. She was high energy and so much fun. She made me laugh, pretty much every time we hung out together, which was often. She usually visited us, but I went over to her parents' house from time to time. They had a lovely dairy and alpaca farm. I enjoyed watching the alpacas playing in the fields together, such sweet animals. My favorite was a girl with light brown fur and the most soulful eyes named Belinda. Such an affectionate girl whenever someone petted and talked to her. An absolute sweetheart.

Robin had horses too. I had taken riding lessons as a child and rode horses in my early twenties for a time. Getting back into riding exhilarated me. Sitting atop a beautiful, strong horse, galloping across the fields, wiped away any worries plaguing me at the time. I was free and living in the moment.

Today, July 23rd, was opening day for Poplin Fresh, my little market. Archie and I had stocked the shelves yesterday and everything was ready to go. I was a bundle of nerves all night, hoping opening day would go well.

I put my coffee cup in the sink and walked outside. Archie fed the chickens in their coop behind the barn at the right of the house. I watched my feathered girls pecking away at the feed.

"Fourteen eggs today," he said, walking out of the coop holding a full basket. "These chickens lay a lot of eggs."

"Lucky for us," I remarked. "Let me clean them off; I'll take them to the store with me."

"I'll do it, I'm going with you anyway," he said. "Can't miss opening day."

"If you insist." I smiled, following him inside.

I walked around the store, arranging things, making sure everything looked just right. Bright strawberries, plump blueberries, carrots, tomatoes, peas, green beans, and cucumbers filled the display areas. The refrigerated case was fully stocked with brown eggs and some strawberry pies I'd made. Another display area showcased my homemade strawberry jam, and assorted fruit pies, apple, cherry, and blueberry.

"This is it," I said to Archie excitedly. I unlocked the front door and looked at him expectantly. Nobody came in. I hadn't expected a big rush, of course, but I had hoped for a few people to be excited about the store opening.

"Don't worry." Archie gave me a hug. "People will come." I saw his kind eyes, desperate to ease my disappointment, or distract me from it. "This summer is going so fast. In two weeks, I'll be getting my classroom ready."

I laughed. I'd take the change of subject. "Crazy, right? Everything is coming together. I..." My gaze traveled to the refrigerated case. Something didn't look right.

"What's wrong?" Archie asked.

I opened the case and picked up a familiar bag of organic dates. Familiar, but not something I'd seen in many years. I held up the bag. "Did you put this in here?"

Archie looked at the bag. "Dates? No, not me."

"Oh, okay," I took the bag to the back room and stared at it, a sinking feeling in the pit of my stomach.

The morning, hazy, hot and humid, a typical July day in Pennsylvania, had yet to reach its heat index as Archie, Robin and I hiked on the Appalachian Trail in the Blue Mountains, not far from our new home.

Archie stopped and took a long drink from his water bottle. "How far is this lookout?"

"Not far," said Robin. She held the leash to her dog, Daisy, a sweet, gray Labrador. Daisy barked, causing us to move farther down the rocky trail under a veil of green maple, oak, and other assorted trees in the forest.

Sweat dripped off my forehead, but I was happy to be on the trail, out in the wilderness, feeling the heartbeat of nature. Robin liked to hike too. She went most weekends and when she invited us to go along, I jumped at the chance, excitement racing through me. I hadn't been hiking for quite a while, but it used to be part of my regular routine. Archie, however, wasn't too thrilled. He enjoyed the outdoors on a limited basis.

He swiped at a fly on his arm. "Seriously, is it much farther?"

Robin laughed and we turned a corner in the woods, an

opening in the trees visible up ahead. In minutes we'd reached it, and were rewarded by a breathtaking panoramic view of the valley. The large, smooth white rocks provided a perfect spot to sit and enjoy the view. Farmland stretched out below us, dotted with houses and barns. Forests spread out among a few large ponds, and the sky above was bright blue punctuated by white, endless fluffy clouds.

The setting, although different, took me back to other hiking experiences, other vistas that spread out before me in such a magnificent way. I closed my eyes for a moment and inhaled. Archie's and Robin's voices drifted away, and I could almost smell the scent of sacred herb in the air. I imagined my body, clothed in a simple white flowing gown, swaying in a hypnotic movement, my hands raised to the heavens. An energy vibrating through me, igniting sensations of a highly conscious state.

"What are you doing?" Archie's voice broke into my self-induced trance.

"What?" I asked. My eyes flew open. My arms were raised high into the air. I was moving my body from side to side as Archie and Robin stared at me. "Um, nothing." I put my arms down and stared at the view.

We sat on the rocks, eating turkey sandwiches and apples, watching hang gliders take off from a grassy runway nearby. The one about to jump off the side of the mountain had a triangle wing of a bright green sailcloth with a neon yellow stripe down the middle. He stood a distance away from the edge of the cliff, then began to run, jumped off the edge, and sailed into the sky, like a bird taking flight.

"Oh, that's cool," Archie remarked. He took a bite of his sandwich, staring at the hang glider.

"Yeah, it is." I turned to Robin. "You ever try it?"

"No." Robin shrugged her shoulders. "That's not for me."

I nodded and bit into my apple, watching the hang glider drift off into the open sky, and sail smoothly through the air, seemingly effortlessly. Like a dream taking flight.

NINE

2016

The Commune
Dream

The warm summer sun filtered through the trees towering over us. Sunny and I lay on a blanket, watching its movement and feeding each other her favorite organic medjool dates. She gave up sugar when she joined the commune, as we all had, preferring to keep our bodies free of its addictive poison; but the sweet dates were her one indulgence and I made sure to always have them for her. Dates were a luxury at Listening Lark, only available to all family members during special times.

The commune was a contradiction sometimes. Freedom to do as you want, yet still rules. Is there anything such as complete freedom? Maybe that depends on how you define freedom and the price you must pay to get it. You can have freedom but not necessarily be free. I think we often think of it as an outward journey, yet the inward journey is the most important, and the most difficult. At least in the commune, our freedom wasn't challenged as it might be in the outside world with regular jobs, rent, taxes and everything else people had to struggle with on a day-to-day basis. Not to mention legal issues that may arise. Oh, I knew all about them.

Sunny, meanwhile, knew about internal forces. I saw her struggles, her inward journey. It was part of what drew us together. A brokenness existed inside her, the same as me, and I felt that pull not only of our bodies, but our hearts as well, maybe to heal that wound and salvage what was left. She didn't tell me much about her past, but I felt there were many details in it that she didn't want to discuss, and that was fine with me. I, too, had many details from my past I chose to ignore. At Listening Lark though, we could forget them, and live in the here and now.

We liked to sit in silence together on occasion; Sunshine Lotus and Dream, together on another plane, I often thought. We smoked the sacred herb, large puffs rising to the tree branches and swirling all around us. We were the only life forms that existed in this state, and I wished this was true always, but even at a commune, you had to face reality at some point.

TEN

2023

Aimee

The day passed in a blur. Despite the slow start, customers eventually arrived, and bought numerous items, making opening day a success. But I could barely feel my happiness; my mind was completely focused on only one thing.

That damn bag of dates.

They still sat on the counter in the back room of the store. I wouldn't take them into my house. Our house. Who would have placed them in the refrigerated case? How could someone get into the store? None of it made any sense to me. But I knew one thing. Those dates were meant for me, not as a snack, but as a warning.

Was it Brother Jim? Had he found me after all these years?

I fiddled around in the barn, scooping chicken feed into a metal bucket. Sweat ran down my forehead. Today was a classic hazy, hot and humid summer day and I longed to jump into the pool to cool off, which I would soon do. I leaned over to get a bigger scoop, the strap of my denim overalls falling off my shoulder. Finally, the bucket was full. I pulled my strap up and headed out to the coop.

The chickens circled for their food, squawking, and pecking as soon as it was dispersed. I laughed at their excitement and gathered all the eggs, which I then took to the slop sink in the barn, washing and drying each egg before placing them into cartons. I would keep them in the small refrigerator until I transported them to the store, minus a couple. Those I needed for breakfast.

Archie had a dentist appointment this morning, so it was just me for breakfast today. I entered the back door into the kitchen and sat the egg carton on the counter. The ceiling fan at the center of the room hummed lending sound to an otherwise silent house. I surveyed the kitchen, everything appeared normal, but my senses heightened and I felt on edge, unsure of my surroundings. I paused, I was used to the quiet by now, but something disturbed me in the familiar space.

Something felt...

Ominous.

I stood still for a few minutes, just listening. Other than the fan, I didn't hear anything, but something nipped at me, an uneasy feeling I was unable to shake off. I scanned the room again, plucking a large knife out of the block on the kitchen counter.

Was someone here?

Inside the house?

The same person who left the dates at the store?

I crept down the hall into the living room—nothing appeared disturbed. Nor in the dining room or small office downstairs. I now stood at the base of the staircase and proceeded up the stairs. I took one step and then stopped, listening again. Was that something? A shuffle of some sort? My heart hammering, I stood still for a few more minutes, but no more sound came. I moved up the stairs slowly, gripping the rich walnut handrail.

I tried to tread as carefully as possible. The stairs showed their age, and it seemed as if each one had a particular squeak. I maintained my breathing and pussyfooted up the stairs, still listening. For what, I wasn't sure, but something was here.

Something that should not be here.

Or someone.

I finally reached the top of the stairs and walked down the hall to the master bedroom, first peeking into the hall bathroom, where luckily the shower curtain was opened because I had been cleaning in there earlier. Nothing unusual there.

Our bedroom door was closed. I stared at the doorknob; I was certain it was open when I went downstairs earlier. We rarely, if ever, closed the bedroom door. Why would we? Archie and I were the only ones who lived here. I gripped the doorknob and turned.

The clock by the side of our bed ticked loudly. Louder than I had ever realized: How hadn't I noticed its intensity before? Then again, the room had never seemed so quiet as it did in this moment. Our bed, a king-size sleigh style, dominated the room and was neatly made up in bright blue wedding ring quilt and matching pillow shams. I looked at the gray wingback chair to the side, at our nightstands, each with a creamy white pedestal lamp, and my bureau with a decorative mirror and wide shelf that housed my perfumes, jewelry box and assorted framed photos of myself and Archie, and at a tall dresser on Archie's side—nothing looked out of place. My gaze fell on my vanity table by the window, filled with makeup, moisturizers, and hair items. Lying in the center of the table was a necklace. A remembrance of long ago. Something that had not been in my jewelry box, but wrapped in a small bag, buried in an old shoebox in my closet with other mementos of the past. I should have thrown it away.

A turquoise necklace.

I'd searched the entire house, barn and garage, but the intruder was nowhere to be found, finished with their task of the day I supposed. Nerves trickled through me for the rest of the day and mounted inside me so much I felt as if I was going to have a panic attack. It had to be Brother Jim. Who else would have a reason to seek me out? I remembered how scared I'd been when I'd first fled Listening Lark, thinking that he would catch up with me. As more and more time had passed I had relaxed. Clearly that was a mistake. But how had he found me? And why play these cat and mouse games with me now? The man I remembered was someone who confronted people directly, not by leaving creepy reminders. None of this made any sense.

I had composed myself by the time Archie arrived home. He didn't know about this part of my past, and I didn't ever want him to know. How would I even start explaining everything to him? What would he think of me if he knew all the truths of my past? I didn't want to take that chance. One bit of mantra from Listening Lark I kept alive was the stance of living in the here and now. Archie didn't need to know about my past; it had no bearing on our lives now, despite this strange intrusion. No, I would handle whatever was going on. I wouldn't drag my loving Archie into it. I knew he'd do anything to protect me, and I appreciated the sentiment, but I could take care of myself. I'd been doing it for years.

I was toiling in the garden, picking green beans, when he arrived home. The sun stood high in the sky; I should have waited for evening shade to pick but I needed to keep busy.

Archie walked out the back door in his swimming trunks, wearing sunglasses. He spotted me in my cut-off denim overalls and wide-brimmed sun hat, squatting down, hurriedly picking beans and adding them to the basket I held.

"Hey, it's too hot for that," he called. "Come swimming with me."

Just the sight of him was enough to start to calm my racing heart. "Okay," I replied, my smile genuine. "I'll just finish this row and I'll put my suit on."

"You don't need a suit," he said.

"You're wearing one," I said, laughing.

"Not for long." He jumped into the pool and threw his suit on the side.

I left the basket full of beans in the dirt and joined my naked husband in the pool.

This was the exact distraction I needed.

ELEVEN

2023

Aimee

Poplin Elementary School was a large tan brick building with a bright red roof. Well-manicured green shrubbery nestled in dark mulch filled the flowerbeds, and bright red geraniums stood in an elegant row in front. Archie and I parked in the back parking lot and entered through the side door. A few other teachers and staff, including Robin, also headed in.

"Ooh, Aimee. I'm so glad you're here," she said, her arms full of tote bags stuffed with random items. "Would you help me set up my back bulletin board before you help Archie? I'm doing a movie theme this year. I already did one board with the students' names, but I still have to do our best work board. Please help me!"

I laughed. "I guess I can for a bit." I turned to Archie. "You'll be on your own for a while, babe."

He smiled as we walked down the hall, its floor gleaming from the summer deep clean. "I think I'll manage."

"Are you doing a movie theme for your classroom, too?" I asked.

"No, I'm doing a camping theme," he said. "Remember all that stuff I ordered?"

"I knew it was for school, but we didn't open anything, so I wasn't sure exactly what it was," I replied. "Camping theme sounds fun."

"Yeah, I brought it all here yesterday, so you have fun in Robin's room and come over when you're done." He opened his classroom door and disappeared inside.

"Yay." Robin grabbed my hand, pulling me into her classroom, across the hall.

The student desks were neatly arranged, five rows, four desks to a row. Each desk had a student's name written on a long pencil design sticker in neat cursive writing. One kidney-shaped table sat in the back of the room stacked with assorted papers, bags, and books. The back wall was lined with student cubbies and coat hooks. To the left was a long table stacked four high with small compartments, marked *iPad Station* on a bright yellow sign on the wall above.

"I can't believe it's only three weeks until the first day of school," Robin remarked, dumping her bag on her desk at the front of the room, by the sink and water fountain. A large poster hung above the sink stating, *Nut-Free Zone.* "And Back-to-School Night is only two weeks away. We have to be ready by then."

"That's what Archie keeps telling me." I pointed to the poster. "Do you have students with nut allergies this year?"

"Oh, not this year, but it's always a nut-free zone in my room," she said. "I have a severe allergy."

"Oh, wow. That can be very serious."

"Yes, but I'm used to it; I always have an EpiPen near me," she replied.

"That's wise." I smiled at her brightly. "So, what do you want me to do?"

"First, let's get some candy bars from the lunchroom," she said, digging change from her purse. "My treat."

"You go ahead," I replied. "None for me. I try not to eat too much sugar."

"Really?" Robin raised her eyebrows.

"Yeah, one sugary item per day, or less," I said. "I made apple pie for dessert tonight, so I'll save my allowance for then."

"Wow, I don't think I could have so much self-control," Robin mused, opening the door. "Be back in a minute."

The door slammed shut, her comment about self-control still in my mind. There was a time I allowed no sugar to enter my body. Myself, and everyone around me, considered it a poison, although I always thought that position was a bit extreme. Anything done in moderation is usually okay, unless you have an allergy, like Robin.

Those days on the commune seemed like a lifetime ago. I was certainly a different person then, naïve, trusting, and unable to see that what a person says is not always their true feeling or intention. I'd had troubles with trust before I joined Listening Lark but my time there only intensified my trust issues. I was so desperate to have someone love me and be a part of a family that I rushed in without a second thought. Now I was willing to trust, but you had to prove your trustworthiness to me first. I considered all my actions first before rushing into a situation.

The classroom door opened and Robin walked inside. "Okay." She held up a half-eaten chocolate bar. "See, no self-control, but I'm ready to begin. Let's tackle this bulletin board."

So, we did. Bright yellow background paper, star cutouts all around the board, movie camera, and large popcorn cutouts on each side of the board and, above, a large sign, bright circles of yellow around the border mimicking stage lights, stating, *Now Showing Our Best Work*, ready for students' creations.

"Looks great," I said, stepping back to admire our work.

"We're a great team," Robin replied. She brushed her long, dark hair out of her eyes. She sighed. "I guess I'd better give you back to Archie. Thanks for helping me."

"You're welcome. Yes, I'm sure he's looking for me," I replied.

"Let me take you out for dinner sometime, to say thanks," Robin suggested.

"Oh, you don't have to do that. It was just a bulletin board, no big deal."

"Not just that. I've really enjoyed spending time with you this summer. Let's celebrate being neighbors."

I smiled. "Okay, sounds fun. Where do you want to go? Poplin Chicken?"

"No, not there. Have you been to Dilly's?" she asked.

I shook my head.

"Tomorrow night, you and me for dinner, girls' night?"

"Sure, sounds fun," I replied, waving goodbye as I walked out her door.

Archie had made progress on his classroom organization while I decorated bulletin boards with Robin. In the back of the room, he'd placed a dark brown area rug, and set up a small green tent with an inflatable campfire in front of it. Dark green round chair cushions sat on the floor around the pretend fire. A camp chair sat to the left of the tent. He now worked on the bulletin board behind the tent.

The board had a black paper background, yellow edging, and *Reading Makes You a Happy Camper* in cutout white letters across the top. Archie stapled some construction pine trees to the bottom of the board.

"Wow, this looks awesome!" I exclaimed. "You've been busy."

He laughed. "Well, I had some of it already set up. Here, help me put the rest of the pine trees and tent on the board."

"Ooh, and stars for the sky," I said, picking up one of the yellow stars sitting on a pile lying on an empty desk.

We stapled the cutouts, stars, trees, and tent, then stood back to admire our work. I was sure his third graders would enjoy our fun bulletin board.

"Not bad," Archie remarked, running a hand through his thick blond hair.

I wrapped my arms around him. "You're not bad," I said, kissing him.

He returned my kiss. I deepened it, pressing my body against his.

"Mmm... you're going to make me want more," he whispered, slightly pulling away.

I held him tight.

"I want more," I said seductively. I nodded over to his desk. "You know, I've never had sex on a teacher's desk."

He smiled. "Oh, really? We can't though, not at school."

I grabbed his hand and led him over to the desk. "Yes, we can. I locked your door and look, I've closed the little curtain on the window."

I pushed his inbox tray and pencil containers to the side and stood at the center of the desk, unzipping my jean shorts and tossing them on the chair.

"So, you planned to seduce me?" he teased, now his hands all over me. My undies are quickly tossed on top of the shorts. He lifted me onto the desk.

"Yes." I laughed. "So much hotter than bulletin boards."

TWELVE

2023

Aimee

Dilly's, a pub-style restaurant, about a thirty-minute drive from Poplin, swarmed with patrons on a busy Friday night. The hostess showed us to a red cushioned booth by the bar, which was lined with men and woman engrossed with their drinks and each other.

"Two merlots," Robin ordered for us. She looked at me. "Right?"

"Yes, sounds good," I agreed, picking up the menu. "So, what's good here?'

"The real question is what was going on in Archie's classroom yesterday? I went over to see you two, but the door was locked, and I heard some... noises inside."

"Hmmm... noises?" I feigned innocence.

"Yeah, not school appropriate noises," she teased. "But seriously, in his classroom?"

"Why not?" I asked. "Makes it more exciting."

"Very interesting," Robin said, laughing.

"You've never had sex in your classroom with a boyfriend?" I asked, grinning.

She laughed again. "No, I've hardly even had a boyfriend in the last year or so."

"Why not?"

"I don't know. Haven't found anyone I'm interested in."

"No online dating?"

"A little, but again, nobody very interesting. It's tough around here. The last guy was so concerned about what his ex-girlfriend was doing, it was all he talked about during the entire date. I don't even know why he wanted to go out with me."

"Yeah, there's a lot of losers out there," I commented.

"But you and Archie, you two are great together."

I smiled. "We are. We really love each other." Sometimes it seemed like a movie the way Archie walked into my life at the right time, almost as if he was waiting to find me. I wouldn't have been ready for a relationship if I had met him earlier. I remembered how my heart raced when this cute guy came into the coffee shop to pick up his large coffee order, and how we flirted with each other. I felt so alive in that moment, more than I had in years.

"How long have you been together?"

"Um... a little over a year. We only dated a few months, we were engaged for a short time and then got married. Things happened so fast for us. When it's right, it's right."

"Oh, wow, that is fast. Did you meet online?"

"Nope, in person. I know, so old-fashioned," I said. "I was working in a coffee shop, and he came in for an order he was picking up for school."

"Really?" Robin's eyes widened. "Love at first sight?"

"I don't know about love, but definitely lust at first sight." I laughed. "The love came a bit later, but not by much."

"One of these days I'll find my Archie; until then I'm happy to enjoy being with myself," replied Robin.

"Good outlook. Time with yourself is always time well spent," I agreed.

The waitress sat two more glasses of merlot in front of us. Our first glasses were still half full.

"Um, we didn't order these," I said.

"But we did order cheese fries as an appetizer," Robin chimed in.

"That guy over there sent the wine over. The fries will be out any minute," the waitress said, first pointing to a guy standing at the bar, then she walked away.

The guy was tall, solidly built, not particularly overweight, but not particularly in shape, either. He had short dark hair, friendly brown eyes and wore a green baseball hat that read *Poplin Hardware*. He was dressed in dark jeans with a large belt buckle, a dark blue short-sleeve button shirt and worn, brown leather cowboy boots.

"Oh, John Larabe," Robin said, and disappointment colored her voice. She waved at him, and he smiled, walking toward our table. "Great, now he's going to come over."

"Who is he?" I asked quickly before he reached us.

"He works at the hardware store in Poplin. He lives in that small ranch house at the edge of town with his grandmother. He does some farming work for the Blauchs and my dad, sometimes."

I nodded. The hardware store was right next to my store, so I imagined I would run into him from time to time.

"Hello, ladies," John greeted us. He held his hand out to me. "John Larabe, nice to meet you."

"Aimee Greencastle," I said, shaking his hand. "My husband and I recently moved to Poplin."

"I know, you bought the Miller farm," he said.

Isn't he a nosy one? I stared at him for a moment before replying.

"Yes, and I hear you work at the hardware store. I just opened a small market next door, Poplin Fresh."

"Yeah, I've been meaning to stop by sometime." He turned to Robin. "And how do you two know each other?"

"Neighbors. You know where I live," Robin said; an edge had crept into her voice. "And her husband will be teaching third grade at the school."

"Oh, I didn't know your husband was a teacher," John remarked, rubbing his chin. "I was talking to him the other day."

"You met Archie?" I asked.

"Just briefly, at the hardware store," he explained. "Before you moved in everyone in town was talking about the rich people from Philly moving in."

I raised my eyebrows and glanced at Robin, who shifted uncomfortably in her seat.

"Well, thank you for the wine, John. That was very kind, but I think we need some time to decide what to order for dinner," Robin said.

"Sure, you're welcome, and, Robin, let me know when you're free, maybe we can go out to dinner again sometime," John replied, flashing a wide smile at her. "Nice to meet you, Aimee." We watched him walk back to the bar.

"That was interesting; what's going on with you two?" I asked. "Go out for dinner *again*?"

Robin blushed. "It's embarrassing. He is not my type at all. I don't know why I even went out with him. It was such a boring date."

"He doesn't seem that bad," I commented. Not that good, either. Just kind of blah. Not my type, and clearly not Robin's either.

Robin looked at me. "You know what I mean. He's not unattractive, but he's not good looking. If he had a great personality that would be something, but he doesn't. Do you know what he talked about on our date? Tractors! On a first date. I can have a conversation about tractors with my father. John is a dead end. There's no way that is happening."

I laughed. "Tractors? Yeah, no thanks. You dodged a bullet on that one."

"Cheese fries, ladies." The waitress placed a large basket of cheesy goodness in front of us.

"Yes!" we both chirped in unison, then laughed, digging into the fries.

THIRTEEN
2016

The Commune
Dream

We lay beneath a star-filled sky on a dark summer night, together as a family. We joined as a group to chant and meditate, basking in Mother Nature's beauty and bounty. Brother Jim was certain we would be able to see Aquarius tonight in the southern sky, which would be a treat because it wasn't always possible by its dimmer stars. Each of us sat upon our light gray cotton sleep sacks and marveled at the scene above us; even though Aquarius hadn't been spotted yet, we welcomed her appearance, chanting in harmony with our fellow family members.

Sunny and I pushed our sleep sacks together to create a comfortable space for us to take pleasure in the night together. The hot, humid mid-July night surrounded us, drips of sweat coming from our bodies no matter how little activity we did, or how few clothes we wore. This time of year, everything felt alive around us, vibrating with energy and fervor. Sunny and I were no exception.

It was hard to remember a time when I felt more alive than this, in the heat of the night, chanting with my brothers and sisters, beside my woman, her heartbeat the same as my own, her sweaty body writhing against mine as we chanted. No, this moment in time proved the magical intensity and action of Listening Lark. I wasn't only living life, I was feeling life, experiencing life. The way a person is intended to do so.

I was life.

Sunny had been angry at me earlier in the day. We'd argued over Moonbeam, one of my former lovers. Sunny hadn't known we had been together, months ago, before I even met Sunny, and now Sunny didn't want the turquoise necklace made by Moonbeam.

I loved to see that necklace on Sunshine Lotus though; it reminded me of the first time we met at the farmers' market. As if the heavens had opened and my fantasy girl appeared among the masses of folks shopping for cantaloupes and ripe tomatoes. When she put that turquoise necklace on, it hung perfectly between her lovely breasts encased in a form-fitting black tank top. I knew she would be mine. Beyond just physical attraction, which vibrated through my body, it was as if lightning had struck, and nothing mattered except her, and me being with her.

We had a long discussion. Moonbeam and I had a strictly platonic relationship now and that is how it would stay. I did not, and would not, want anything else. In fact, Moonbeam was now one of Brother Jim's women. Reminding her of this took away Sunny's worries about her and changed her mind about the necklace.

I may be a dreamer, but I can be very persuasive when I want to be, and today I was rewarded with Sunny's love and trust.

An honor I would always cherish.

FOURTEEN

2023

Aimee

I placed two more egg cartons into the refrigerated case at the store and closed the door. I was careful to monitor every inch of the store for any oddities, like strange bags of dates. Luckily, they hadn't appeared again. Hopefully, things would stay that way.

After finding the turquoise necklace inside my house, I had trouble calming my racing mind. It was one thing finding the dates at the store, but knowing this person had been in my house, in my bedroom going through my things, made me sick.

And scared.

Brother Jim wasn't someone you messed around with. He was a scary guy. I wished I knew why he was here now. And I couldn't figure out why he wouldn't simply confront me because that was his style. I didn't understand any of it. I found myself constantly scanning faces of people in town, searching for Jim, but unsure what I'd do if I saw him.

Thoughts lingered in my mind, the same constant thoughts that plagued me for a long time. I didn't want to make any plans, not yet. I didn't fully know what I was dealing with at this point. I thought I'd left all of this behind me years ago. Why would my past seek me out now?

I went back to the box I'd brought from home and took out the quarts of blueberries, more strawberry jam and blueberry muffins I'd baked the night before. I even had a few onions and potatoes to add to the abundance of tomatoes, carrots, sweet-corn, and cucumbers. My little garden was flourishing, and it gave me a wonderful feeling of satisfaction.

When I was a girl, my mother planted a garden every year and I always helped her plant the seeds and the small plants. I loved putting my hands in the dirt, pressing into the life-giving soil and gathering the fruits of our labor after a few months of growth. It was like a kind of miracle to get food to sustain your body from planting a simple seed. I enjoyed all stages of its growth from seed to harvest.

When my parents died, I forgot about gardening. I forgot about everything. I went to live with Aunt Lou, and she tried to help me, but she didn't understand. And neither did I.

I rediscovered the love of Mother Earth and all its bounty a couple years later. The growth, the freedom, the love, the ability to just live in the moment, only the here and now. Such a tranquil existence. Until it wasn't.

I shook off my uncomfortable thoughts. The truth was, for so long I could never imagine living a life like the one Archie and I were creating in Poplin. Living a simple life, but a real one, with boundaries, trust, and room to grow and expand. A grown-up life. This was a life I never realized I wanted until I could see it in my grasp. I wouldn't allow anything, or anyone, to take it from me.

The front door opened, and John Larabe walked in.

"Hello, John," I greeted in a friendly tone.

"Hi, Aimee. I told you I'd stop in sometime," he replied, with a smile.

"You sure did," I said, adding the blueberry muffins, individually wrapped, to the display.

"Those look really good," he remarked. "I'll take four of those."

"Okay, I'll put them by the register," I said. "Just take your time and look around."

"Sure," he replied.

I busied myself with the muffins and then tidying up my boxes and bags from the checkout area, moving them to the back room. I washed my hands in the bathroom sink and went back out to arrange my jams on the shelf.

"Nice store," John remarked. He added a quart of blueberries, carrots, and two jars of strawberry jam to the muffins already sitting on the counter. He pointed to a bench that sat toward the front of the store. "Who made that?"

"Archie. The previous owners of the farm left some woodworking equipment behind in the barn, so he started making benches. He used to help his grandpa with woodworking projects quite a bit. They came out well. We have two on our front porch, and two in the barn. I thought I'd bring it in and see if it sells."

John walked over to the bench and lifted the price tag. He nodded. "I'll take it. He did a nice job on it."

I nodded and was going to say something but stopped. John's attention had diverted to something outside. He walked over to the front window and stared. While he was distracted, I stared at him. I understood why Robin didn't want to date him, even beyond the tractor talk. There was something judgmental about him, unnerving, even though it wasn't something that came through in an obvious fashion, but rather a vibe, an energy I felt from him. A feeling that settled over you when you didn't particularly like someone, but are not sure why, certainly not for a reason you could state. I didn't trust him.

"What's going on outside?" I asked.

John shrugged. "Oh, nothing. Just someone I wanted to talk to, but I'll catch up with them later." He walked up to the checkout counter.

"Okay, so you want the bench; that will make Archie's day," I said, walking over to the register. I rung up the rest of his purchases.

"Tell him it will be sitting on my front porch," John said.

"Oh, I will," I replied.

"So, did you and Robin have a good time Friday night?" he asked, his gaze squarely on me.

"Oh, yeah, we had fun," I said. "The food was good. I had the chicken marsala."

"Yes, that is good there," he agreed. "Maybe when Robin and I go out again, I'll take her there."

I nodded, unsure of how to respond. I placed his groceries in a paper bag. He swiped his card, and I handed him his bag and receipt.

"Thanks for stopping in; do you need help with the bench?" I asked.

"Nope, I got it." He walked over and easily picked it up.

"Great, enjoy the rest of your day."

"Thanks, same to you. I'm off from the hardware store today, but I'll be cutting hay later."

"Oh, that's right, Robin mentioned that you farmed too?"

"Did she?" His eyes brightened. "Yeah, Archie asked the other week if I'd be interested in doing your fields. You have corn and alfalfa, right?"

"Oh... yes we do," I replied. Surprised that Archie hadn't mentioned this to me. And I never should have told him what Robin said about him; now he knew we'd talked about him. She wouldn't be happy with that.

"Anyway, you'll see me later at your house."

"Oh, all right."

"Okay, great," said John, picking up his bag. "Have a good one."

I nodded, watching him walk out the door. I grabbed my phone and typed a text to Archie.

> So, John Larabe is doing our alfalfa fields today?

Three dots.

> Great.

Three dots.

> I told you about that, right?

> No, why didn't you?

> Sorry, babe. I must have forgot.

I sighed. It wasn't a big deal, but annoying.
Three dots.

> Sorry. 🖤

He is sweet.

> OK, just keep me in the loop.

> Always.

I laughed. Then typed.

> Hey, I sold your bench.

> Awesome, to who?

> John.

I sat my phone down. It was probably good that John could take care of the fields, but Archie needed to communicate with me when it involved the store or the farm. I was in charge of the finances for those areas, while Archie took care of our personal finances. We were equal partners in everything, but I got the feeling Archie felt a little weird about our money when we first got married because I brought so much more of it into the marriage, due to the large inheritance received from Aunt Lou, so I thought splitting the responsibilities would be a good idea. So far it had seemed to work: Archie was more comfortable with everything, and now with buying the property we were part-ners, in marriage and everything.

Another text popped up on my phone. Robin.

> Are you at home?

> No, I'm at the store. Why?

Three dots.

> I'm at your house. There is music playing inside. I thought you couldn't hear me knock.

I stared at the phone, then looked at the clock hanging on the wall over the cash register. Archie could be back from doing errands, but he said he got a late start today. Unless someone else turned on the music. I typed.

> I'm not there. I must have left the music on. Just go home. I'll catch up with you later.

No response. Five minutes passed.

Worry filled me. Little stabs of fear poked relentlessly into me. What if Brother Jim broke into our house again, assuming it was him? What if Robin somehow got into the house? He wasn't someone Robin could handle. She better just leave. I stared at my phone. *Please respond.*

A text came up on my phone.

No, I'll come by the store. See you soon.

A sigh of relief escaped me, catching me by surprise. Robin was becoming a friend to me. A real friend that I cared about and enjoyed spending time with, doing whatever. It had been a long time since I had a friend. I worried about her, which was unusual for me. This town was changing me. And whoever was lurking around from my past had to go.

I'd make sure of it even though I was scared as hell.

FIFTEEN

2016

The Commune
Dream

Grandmother's house, a midsize 1920s gem, sat on a few acres in the mountains of Santa Monica, hidden behind tall sycamores, cottonwoods, and bay trees. Lemon, orange, and lime trees also inhabited the property. I remembered visiting here as a child and always picked an orange from the young tree off the back patio. Now that orange tree towered over the house, heavy with juicy fruit.

When she died and we inherited the property, Jim Bob transformed into Brother Jim, and brought his small group of followers here, from his apartment in the Valley. After having a long, intense conversation with me, about his vision and plans for the Listening Lark commune, I became smitten with the idea. I'd just gotten out of a complicated situation and needed a fresh start. A place that accepted me, regardless of my past, or future mistakes, plus Jim Bob needed me to be on board. I was fine with him running things without getting in my way. He was fine with me doing as I pleased if I stayed out of his way. A simple partnership that worked for both of us. And I liked Brother Jim's theories, if not always his tactics.

In the commune's early beginnings, we both agreed on the approach to a free lifestyle. No judgment, just living and producing as a unit. A utopia for us and all the Listening Lark family members. Lately, though, we had more disagreements. I didn't like Brother Jim's penchant for control, particularly with some of the female family members. And while he had a few members who contributed substantial money to Listening Lark, he kept a strict regulation on food that was purchased for meals, encouraging our sustainability through gardening, our chicken coop, and fruit trees. All wonderful in theory, but not enough to feed forty people every day. I had a suspicion he was putting money away somewhere, without my knowledge, and that he only showed me a fraction of what Listening Lark brought in. But I didn't want to deal with it. I was comfortable, certainly not lacking in any area. I received my monthly payment from Jim Bob. Brother Jim liked my easy-going personality but hated my lackadaisical approach to life, always had; we clashed from time to time but always came around. We were family.

While all were welcome into our family, I sometimes felt that Brother Jim had an eye for those who could help us to further our mission with financial support. His plans, our plans, for Listening Lark went well beyond the current state, but those plans would require money. A great deal of money.

Listening Lark was lovely. But the three-bedroom house was not large enough to accommodate all of us, so small cabins and tents were constructed all over the property. Sunny and I had a cabin in the back of the house, right under a large orange tree. Simple structures created by River, a strong craftsman, large enough for a queen-size air mattress, a long shower rod to hang our clothing, and four shelves by the arched door opening for miscellaneous personal storage. A comfortable patio chair sat in the corner of the structure. And in the other corner a tiny electric heater shaped like a clay pot to warm us on chilly evenings. We painted the inside of the cabin a creamy white, and River painted a mural of a waterfall on the wall opposite our bed, which was covered in mint green sheets and a white comforter. The combination of white and green gave the small space a relaxing feel. We used the downstairs bathroom in the house, only a few steps away. I could have had a room in the house but chose not to. I preferred living outdoors. Sunny might have preferred to live indoors, but I never told her I had a choice.

One of my favorite things to do was to pick two fresh oranges in the morning and lie in bed with Sunny, peeling and eating the fruit, juices running down our mouths, fingers sticky. It was inevitable that our lips would meet, both juicy and sticky, the sweet nectar of our love marking a glorious new day at Listening Lark.

Sunny and I traveled up Mulholland in the van and turned into the parking lot of the recreation area. We were going to the mountains for a picnic, just the two of us. We loved all our brothers and sisters, but sometimes you didn't want anyone else around. So, when we felt like this, we packed a picnic basket and headed for a trail.

We walked for a time then found a secluded grassy area shaded by a grove of cottonwood trees. Sunny spread out the red blanket she held, and I placed the picnic basket on it. I sat down and she joined me, leaning against my body.

"Perfect spot," she remarked.

I smoothed her hair down her neck and kissed the top of her head. "You're perfect."

We enjoyed the quiet and being together for some time, just listening to birds chirp and the occasional branch breaking in the distance.

"I'm hungry," Sunny said, opening the picnic basket. She retrieved the wine and corkscrew, giving it to me to open while she lifted out the plate of cheese, crackers, and fruit.

"Oh, you put my dates in here too." She smiled. "You know what I like."

"Yes, I do." I laughed.

I popped the cork and poured two paper cups for us and we munched on the food. I grabbed a date and put it on Sunny's lips. She opened her mouth and grabbed it from my hand.

"I'm so glad I found you," she said. "What would I be doing if we never met?"

"You'd be at UCLA, fighting off all the frat guys," I said.

She laughed. "How do you know I'd be fighting them off?"

"I don't think frat boys are your type."

"They're not," she said.

"I never have been happier with anyone else," I told her. "Nobody compares to you."

"I feel the same." She paused. "You know I hold a lot inside of me. Emotions and stuff from the past."

"I know. I feel it, and if you want to, we can talk about it, but I don't think you do."

She looked at me. "I don't, not now, maybe not ever, but you knowing that without me having to tell you is what I love about you, Dream."

"Well, I love everything about you, Sunny," I said, kissing her.

Love isn't something you plan on, but when it's real, it's everything. I thought I'd found love in the past, but that relationship had gotten messy, messier than what I wanted or expected. I was a different man now. A man of balance and meditation. Calmness and thought. I wouldn't allow anger and darkness to lead me down its tight, narrow path. I had light now.

I had Sunny.

SIXTEEN

2023

Aimee

Relief flooded me when Robin walked through the door of my store, her high ponytail bouncing, a bright smile on her pretty face. I was so glad she had decided not to investigate what was happening inside our house.

"I'm glad to see you," I greeted her.

"You too," she replied. "So, yeah, you must have left music on or the TV on at your house. I don't think Archie was home. I texted him too, but he didn't answer."

"No, he went to Elmville this afternoon. Needed to get something to fix the sink in the laundry room; it's leaking. The hardware store here didn't have the part. And we need chicken feed and some things for the barn too. He'll be gone for a while," I explained.

She nodded, and I busied myself arranging my assorted jams. A few more customers had purchased jars in the past half hour, and they were a bit askew. I was a stickler for order in some ways, a big departure from my former self. Plus, I could let my mind wander about the music playing in our house. It was possible that Archie had left the TV on, possible. Or someone else was inside the house.

Waiting for me.

Knowing I wasn't home.

Playing games with me.

Like old times.

I sighed. I didn't want Archie to get home before me. I glanced at the clock. I probably had another hour or so until he got back from Elmville. Maybe I'd close the store early and head home. Noise broke through my thoughts and I realized Robin was talking to me.

"Do you and Archie want to go to the fair with me tomorrow?" She looked at me expectantly.

"The fair?" I asked.

"Yes, tomorrow, it's the first day of the Poplin Area Fair. It's at the fairgrounds on the edge of town. It's nothing much. Some agriculture displays, animal judging contests, games, a couple carnival rides, lots of great food. I love the milkshakes."

"Okay, sure," I agreed. "What time?"

"I'll pick you up around five."

"Sure, that works," I said, turning away from the jam. "Your boyfriend was in here earlier by the way."

Robin raised her eyebrows.

"John," I said.

Robin scrunched her face. "Ugh, don't call him that. Definitely not my boyfriend."

"I know, just teasing you," I replied. "He is going to be harvesting our fields though."

"Better yours than mine," she quipped. We both laughed.

"Okay, well, I have some phone calls to make; is that all you wanted?" I asked, trying to hurry her along.

"Oh, here." She handed me a grocery bag. I peeked inside to see a stack of empty egg cartons. "You said you were running low on cartons, and my mom has saved egg cartons for years."

I laughed. "Thank you!"

She turned to walk out the door. "See you tomorrow."

She waved and the door closed behind her. I quickly went to lock it and put up the closed sign. Then I grabbed my purse and hurried out the back door to my car.

I pulled my car into the garage but didn't hit the button to close it. Archie's car was gone, so he wasn't home yet. I held my house keys in my hand and paused outside the side door that led into a newly added laundry room. A few birds continued to chirp outside and dogs barked far away. A soft breeze rippled the tall, green corn standing all around our house—the perfect camouflage for someone to hide in and watch from afar. My eyes darted around me as I listened for the music Robin had heard earlier, or any other unusual sounds, and my other hand gripped the pocketknife I always kept in my purse, sharpened and ready to bite, if needed. All I heard were the earlier sounds, nothing out of place.

The house remained silent. I inserted the key into the lock and turned. The door creaked open, and I entered, closing it behind me. Stepping lightly onto the tan linoleum floor, I passed the washer and dryer and entered the kitchen. A lingering aroma of coffee hung in the air. That couldn't still be from this morning. I walked over to the deep farmhouse sink. A single blue stoneware mug sat in the center. The long, curved, stainless-steel sink faucet dripped, echoing in the otherwise quiet room. I pushed back the handle to stop it.

Silence enveloped me.

I stood still, again trying to pick up on any unusual sounds. A thump, a rustling, any movement indicating I was not alone.

None came.

I walked through the hallway into the living room. The large flat screen hung above the fireplace, dark and still.

Nothing out of place on the sofas or recliner by the fireplace. I traveled up the squeaky stairway to the second floor, holding on to the wide walnut handrail.

I placed a sandaled foot onto the top of the landing, recently buffed walnut hardwood floor gleaming in the hallway. My other foot moved to join the first when a sound stopped me.

A faint tinkling.

From the attic.

I stood still, listening. Silence. Then another tinkling above me. It occurred to me I hadn't checked the attic when the necklace appeared on my vanity table.

Was someone waiting for me upstairs?

Shivers raced through me. I steeled my body. If they were waiting, I was ready to fight, if I had to do so. I walked to the attic door at the end of the hallway. My hand reached out to turn the doorknob.

Another sound stopped me.

A loud knocking at the front door.

I turned and crept down the stairs, quietly sidling up to sneak a look through the peephole.

A man in a baseball cap and a plaid blue short-sleeve shirt stood on the other side of the door.

John Larabe.

I opened the door.

"Hey, John," I greeted. "I feel like I just saw you." I laughed awkwardly at my dumb joke.

He gave me an odd smile.

"Yeah, just wanted to let you know I'm here to do the fields."

I nodded, noting the large John Deere tractor in our side field. "Great." I paused. "That's a big tractor."

He nodded. "Yes."

"Um... what if someone was in the field and that tractor went through it?"

A confused look crossed his face. "Do you think someone is in the field?"

I shook my head. "No, I just wondered."

"Well, if someone is hiding in the field, they better get out. This tractor could do serious damage to a person if they got caught in it," he stated.

"I would imagine," I replied. "Okay, thanks for letting me know. Bye."

I closed the door. Maybe harvesting the field would have a dual benefit. I stared at the landing on the second floor. I mounted the stairs, taking two at a time, a firm grip on my pocketknife until I was once again at the attic door.

I turned the knob.

I entered the dark, narrow stairway, not sure if I should pull the string light or just scurry up the stairs and look around.

Another tinkling. Louder now that I was in the stairwell. I scurried. Now I stood at the top, dark, musty attic surrounding me.

Tinkle.

A wooden wind chime hung from the ceiling, directly in front of the stained-glass window at the center of the house. The window stood slightly ajar, allowing a breeze to enter the room, moving the wind chime. I pulled the string light in the center of the room.

Its dim light gave a bit more clarity to the few shapes in the room. An old trunk of Aunt Lou's filled with photo albums and assorted memorabilia of our family. Two of Archie's filing cabinets. Two old wooden rocking chairs, an old Tiffany lamp, and a stunning walnut wardrobe that likely weighed a ton and nobody wanted to move, that were left from the previous owners. I opened the wardrobe door. Empty as it had been when we moved in. Nothing looked any different than that day.

The wind chime. I didn't remember it. Did Archie hang it?

Why would he do that though? And why was the window open?

I surveyed the attic again, nothing unusual. I walked to the window, casting a glance below before closing it.

John Larabe stood in the yard.

Staring back at me.

SEVENTEEN

2023

Aimee

I stared out the passenger side window of Robin's car, air conditioning blasting in my face, a cool reprieve before arriving at the fair. I glanced back at Archie in the backseat, scrolling through his phone. Yesterday, after John left the yard to do the fields, I scoured the house again, but found nothing unusual. My fears had been settled when Archie came home though. I told him what Robin said about hearing music in the house, and he said he'd been watching TV with a coffee. He didn't see her text until later. He also confirmed the wind chime was there when we moved in, and that he opened the attic window on occasion to air it out. Mystery solved. John staring at me from the front lawn? The guy was a weirdo, that much I knew.

It didn't explain everything though. The dates and the necklace were another matter. Reminders of the past, but were they threats? Were they indications that someone, likely Brother Jim, wanted to hurt me? I couldn't be sure, but it seemed doubtful. If entering my house and store was so easy, they could have already inflicted harm. But the question of why now still haunted me every time I analyzed the situation. Years had passed since my time at Listening Lark, and how could someone have found me here? There'd been no marriage announcement, I had a different last name now, why now and how? Why not just be direct and confront me, especially if it was Brother Jim, which was my best guess. Why do all of these cloak and dagger scenarios by leaving me reminders of the past? Sure, it was creepy, but what did it accomplish, other than making me uncomfortable? The more I thought about it, the more certain I became that this individual wanted more than that from me. But what?

Robin pulled off the road and drove along a stone lane. A man wearing a neon orange vest directed her to park in the grass beside a gigantic blue truck with dual wheels and large headlights on the top.

"Oh, great," she remarked, parking the car.

"What?" I asked.

She pointed to the truck. "That's John's truck."

"Oh," I said. "Yeah, I could see him driving something like that. A bit over the top?"

"Ridiculous," she replied. "And it's so loud. He thinks it's cool."

I laughed. "Funny what some people think is cool."

We got out of her car and rounded the truck. John was a few feet ahead of us, so we hung back, taking our time, except Archie.

"I'm going to catch up with John," he said. "I want to ask him something."

We waved him away and continued to walk very slowly, as it was obvious Robin wanted to avoid any conversation with him. I wasn't particularly interested in talking to him either. Now fair food, that was another story.

"Hey, let's go get funnel cake," I suggested. We made a beeline for the funnel cake stand. A few minutes later, funnel cake in one hand, fresh squeezed lemonade in the other, we searched for a place to sit down. A row of picnic tables under a shady maple tree was our choice.

I scooped up a piece of powdered sugar delight and shoved it in my mouth. Mmmm... it had been a long time since I ate fair food. It was *so* good.

"You're eating sugar today," Robin remarked; powdered sugar clung to her lips.

"Oh, yeah, the food is the main objective of any fair," I replied. "I mean, what else do you do at a fair?"

"Right on," she agreed. "Hey, look." She pointed to the center of the picnic table where a flyer had been stapled. A picture of our realtor, Angela, smiling, wearing a dark blue dress, her hair neatly done, a friendly smile directed at the camera, was in the center of the flyer. Twenty-five-thousand-dollar reward for any information leading to the arrest of her killer.

"Wow." I stared at the paper. "I wonder if they have any leads."

Robin nodded. "I heard they are looking for a white Honda, four doors. Someone noticed it driving back along the lane of the property she was showing the day she was murdered. Didn't think it was odd at the time, but called the police after hearing about the murder."

"Where was the property again?" I asked.

"Jasmine Road, just past the feed mill. It's very secluded. Long lane, and a lot of trees, no neighbors for a mile or two."

"That's right. Archie was telling me it was past the school and down much farther."

"Right." Robin took a drink of lemonade. "I hope they find who did this. Still, no real leads, or motive, that we know of, at least."

"She was obviously targeted. Maybe someone from her

past?" I suggested. I knew all too well how the past continued to follow some people.

"Maybe she had dark secrets that nobody knew about," Robin said cryptically.

I nodded. "Maybe those secrets caught up with her."

The hot summer night passed as we played some carnival games, coin toss and balloon darts, ate all kinds of junk food, fresh cut fries, juicy cheeseburgers and chocolate milkshakes. I drew the line when Archie walked over to the fried Oreo booth. No thanks.

We even took a ride on the rickety Ferris wheel, barely moving as we traveled to the top. I don't know why I even got on the contraption. I hated heights and gripped Archie's hand tightly until we reached the ground again. My wonderful husband held me gently, his presence calming me better than any drug. Part of my issue was the person I saw at the cotton candy stand while we were waiting in line for the ride. The man who stood with his back to us, long flowing dark hair and a loose white shirt, seemed too familiar to me. Brother Jim? Then he turned and I didn't recognize him. I was getting paranoid.

Now we sat on a large blanket in an open field, a wide black sky above us dotted with white twinkling stars. We sipped milkshakes, our second ones of the night.

"Perfect night for fireworks," Archie remarked. "Endless stars."

"So much different than the city skyline," I replied.

Archie grew up in the Old Kensington area of Philly. He was a city kid. Living in a rural area like Poplin was much different than he was used to, but he loved it. All the space, the wildlife—two deer walked through our yard this morning—everything here appealed to him. I was so glad. I knew country life was for me, but I didn't know until now if it was for him. Thankfully, he was willing to give it a try for me and enjoyed living this lifestyle together.

"Room for one more?" a voice asked. We look up to John's smiling face.

"Sure, buddy," Archie said, moving closer to me. "Have a seat."

"Thanks." John sat next to him. Robin sat next to me and nudged my arm. I raised my eyebrows.

The field was a sea of bright colored blankets, children running around, parents trying to quiet them, and couples cuddling close under the moonlight.

"Fields looked good," Archie said to John. "When will you do the rest?"

"Probably finish the alfalfa fields on Monday after work," John replied. "The cornfields will be beginning of September. They had a late start this year."

Archie nodded. "Sounds good. I love looking at the farmland when everything is cut. It's so vast."

"Yeah, I wouldn't live anywhere else," John agreed, sneaking a glance at Robin. "This is the place where I'll marry and have kids. I love it here."

I nudged Robin, but she didn't look my way, avoiding John's remark. Fireworks popped in the sky, taking my attention away from her and John's words, obviously directed at her. A brilliant display of red, blue, and white lighting up the dark humid night.

The crowd silenced as the fireworks captured their full attention. Pop. Pop. Pop.

I wondered if that was the last thing Angela heard.

She was killed by three gunshots, according to the news.

Pop. Pop. Pop.

EIGHTEEN

2016

The Commune
Dream

Brother Jim was a well-muscled man, his workout routine one he followed religiously, of average height with an early receding hairline, long, dark hair that hung past his shoulders, and cunning eyes, who looked older than his thirty years. What he lacked in looks he made up for in charm and speaking skills, a charismatic individual who could talk you into almost anything, and for some people, absolutely anything.

I had the looks, at least that's what everyone in our family said, and girls always preferred me to Jim Bob, but I am five years younger than him. What I didn't have were the people skills, the manipulative ways he possessed. When I was younger it angered me that he could talk his way out of most situations, even though at times this benefited me, as well. As we aged, I realized that anger didn't serve me well and I chose to embrace what his skills brought to me, instead of being jealous. This was a much more optimal state of being in my world. Even though Jim Bob and I were cousins, in many ways we were almost brothers. Grandmother raised both of us right here in this house during different periods of time when our parents weren't around to care for us. Sometimes only him, sometimes only me, and sometimes we lived here together, as we did now. We didn't always get along, then or now ups and downs are normal for any family.

Today the family planted carrots, tomatoes, and peppers in the garden, adding to our already lush Eden. Gardening was Sunny's passion. She loved getting her fingers into the soil, lovingly placing a delicate life source into the ground. When I attended Berkeley, years ago, I studied Philosophy. In a way I found its teachings intertwined with the act of gardening. Belief in something so minuscule in the beginning, some barely a seed, or an idea, depending on which subject, and confidence that the tiny speck will develop into a blooming plant, or thought, producing bounty for you and others. Doesn't this show the truth in both an intellectual and physical state? Every good thing in life starts with a thought and then the follow-up causes said thought to become a reality. There may be no strong logic in the beginning, only a lingering thought which does not diminish, urging us on to create, or initiate creation, of something beautiful.

Brother Jim watched us planting in the expanded garden from his second-story bedroom. Nobody else noticed him as they were busy with the task at hand, and he stood back from the window, so his presence wasn't obvious. I felt his beady eyes boring into me.

And I stared back at him.

NINETEEN

2023

Aimee

Archie and I sat at the kitchen table eating western omelets and fresh fruit for breakfast. I speared a chunk of honeydew and mindlessly chewed it. Archie's phone beeped.

"Who's that?" I asked.

He read the text. "John. He's stopping by to help me fix that leaky sink."

I raised my eyebrows. "You two are becoming best friends."

He laughed, his eyes crinkling. "Kind of like you and Robin."

"I like her," I replied.

"What's the deal between her and John? Things seemed a little odd between them."

"They went out once. He wants to go out again, but she's not interested."

"Why not? Is there something wrong with him?"

I pondered the question. Was there? I'd been thinking about this since I met John and still didn't know the answer. Archie certainly didn't seem to have any hesitation about him. I wasn't exactly thrilled he would be in our house later today. Maybe I hadn't given the guy a chance though, and I was judging him too harshly.

"She's just not into him," I said. "You know how it is. You either have a connection with someone, or you don't."

He nodded. "I guess that's true. Oh, there was news about Angela's murder on the news this morning. You were in the shower when it was on."

"What?"

"It seems she had a relationship with a married man in Elmville for the past year. They're questioning him and his wife."

"Really?" My interest piqued. "Anything else?"

"That's it for now," he said. "So, at least if it was affair-related there's no psycho wandering around killing people in town."

I took a bite of omelet. "Thank goodness. A psycho is the last thing this town needs."

The early evening sky, streaked with pink and white, stretched out above me as I stood up, arching my back, after being hunched over for so long picking green beans. The loud trill of tree frogs surrounded me in the otherwise calm evening. Nature can be noisy in its own special way.

The beans were out of control, so much more bountiful than any other I'd planted in the past. Locals said Pennsylvania soil in this area was especially rich for farming. I guess that was why we were experiencing such a harvest. Not that I was complaining.

A sweetness lingered in the air. Honeysuckle grew wild behind the garden, filling the area with its fragrance. I moved my limbs to the sky, soaking in the oxygen of Mother Earth and feeling her vibrancy racing through my strong body. I felt energized, like I was one with the nature surrounding me. Peace flickered inside me. One of the most important elements in life to me? Peacefulness.

Some say love is the most important and powerful emotion one can experience in life and while I do agree love is integral to a satisfying human experience, I'd venture to say peacefulness has far more importance.

Peace within yourself. Peace in your environment. Peace with those around you. Peace allows you to slow down, listen and absorb what is in your world and how you can relate to the world. It gives you the power to contemplate, plan, and act on ideas swirling in your mind. Peace gives you clarity. I'd lived without peace for too many years to know how important it is to cultivate and nurture.

I bent over to attend to the beans once more. I only had one row left to do. I'd keep a bowl for our refrigerator and the rest would go to the store with me tomorrow to sell. I was on my own tonight. Archie had Back-to-School Night and wouldn't be home until after nine.

Today had been cloudy, so evening seemed to descend earlier than normal. I hurried down the last row, finally putting the last of the beans in my bushel basket. I plopped down in the grass behind the garden, facing the back of our house, and began cleaning them, snapping the ends of the beans off, breaking them in half and placing them into the large bowl I'd brought out from the kitchen.

Lightning bugs began to appear, their small lights dotting the darkening sky. I snapped beans and admired our home. The hayfields to the left were neatly cut, thanks to John, but the right side and along the back of the yard was surrounded by tall corn-stalks with deep green leaves; while Archie enjoyed the vast views when all the fields were cut, I rather liked the closed in, cozy feeling the tall corn afforded to us. Just Archie and I in our little nest.

I expected we would grow old here in our farmhouse, on our land. Maybe we would have children one day. We weren't ready yet, but who knew what the future held for us. Maybe it would just be us; the thought of children wasn't something I was sure I wanted, after my childhood. I was certain I wanted to be here though, in this place, with Archie. Thirty years from now would I still be sitting on the grass on a humid summer night snapping green beans and watching lightning bugs light up the sky? I hoped so.

I stared at our house; only the kitchen light was on and the patio light outside, the rest of the structure shrouded in darkness. An owl hooted in the distance, breaking into the silence of the evening. I continued to snap beans, my bowl almost full.

A coldness rippled through my body, despite the stagnant heat of the night. Goosebumps prickled my arms, and an awareness came over me. I lifted my eyes.

A light was shining from the attic window.

I dropped the beans I held and stood up. The round, white, spider web attic window had been dark only a few minutes before, but now it held a dim light, bright enough for the entire intricate design of the window to be seen.

My heart stilled.

Who was in the attic?

I jabbed my hands into my denim overalls, pulling out my pocketknife. I hesitated. Did I really want to confront whoever it was? I pulled out my phone and texted Archie.

> Will you be home soon?

Three dots.

> Ten minutes.

> Okay, I'll meet you outside.

???

I didn't answer. I'd talk to him when he got home. I looked up from my phone.

The window was dark again.

I stared and trembled. What was going on? I just saw a light on inside the attic. I was sure of it. It wasn't my imagination.

I stayed in the yard, staring at the house and waiting for Archie to arrive home. Finally, headlights came up the lane. I hurried to the garage.

"You have to check the house!" I told him. "There is someone in the attic! There was a light on and now there's not. Someone is in there!"

"Woah slow down, okay, don't worry, babe," he said in a calm voice. "I'll check it out. Are you okay?"

I followed him inside the house and grabbed a knife from the kitchen.

"Take this with you," I whispered.

"Okay," he said, giving me an odd look, but he took the knife and went upstairs.

I debated following him or staying downstairs. I decided to go to the second floor but did not follow him up the attic stairs.

We locked eyes before he pulled the string to light the dark stairway leading to the attic. I gripped my pocketknife and stood at alert in the hallway, listening to every sound in the house.

Archie's footsteps creaked above me. He slowly moved across the room, then silence. I strained to hear anything. Nothing but the tick tock of the hallway clock.

The minutes ticked by. Then, Archie's footsteps traveled down the attic stairs.

I raised my eyebrows. "Well?"

Archie wiped his forehead. "Nothing, except I walked into a spider web."

"Are you serious?" I brushed past him and ran up the stairs.

I pulled on the light string and surveyed the area. Nothing looked any different. I walked over to the wardrobe and looked behind it, seizing the door handles, poking my head inside. Thankfully, nobody was in there.

I turned off the light and traveled back down the stairs to Archie, who now stood waiting in the hall.

"Nothing, right?" he asked.

I raised my eyebrows. "No, but we're checking every inch of the house right now."

"Are you sure you saw a light?" he asked gently. "Could have been something weird like moonlight streaming in from the front window and it looked like a light in the back window."

"Then why did it go off?" I asked.

Archie shrugged. "Maybe the moon moved. I don't know. Look, let's check everything out so you feel better."

So, we did. Every nook and cranny of the house was examined by us, even the damp stone-walled basement under the house. Nothing and nobody was discovered. Thankfully.

Later, after we locked up the house, showered, and Archie quickly drifted off to sleep, I lay wide awake in bed staring at the ceiling. All I could think about was the attic above and the light shining through the spider web window.

I did not imagine the light.

Someone was playing games.

Again.

"Maybe we should install a security system," Archie suggested.

We were in bed and I was still talking about the light in the attic. I woke Archie up because I had to talk about it. No way that was the moon shining through the windows. I knew Archie thought I was being crazy about this, but I saw the light—he didn't.

"I don't know," I replied. "I hate the idea of having cameras installed in our house. I really hate it."

"But then we could see what was going on." He paused. "I don't care for the idea either, but maybe just a Ring camera on the front and back door?"

I mused on the idea. "Okay, but anyone that's sneaking into the house isn't coming through the front door, or the back door, since we keep those locked, but I guess it's a start. We need to check all the windows too, to make sure they are securely locked."

"I'm on it," he agreed. "Then we can see everything on our phones."

Cameras tracking our every move. I absolutely detested the idea. I didn't want cameras surrounding my home, as if I lived in a prison. But I saw his point, especially with all the odd things happening lately. I still hadn't mentioned that I had a good idea of who was doing these things, but I didn't want Archie involved if I could help it. If he installed cameras, then he would have so many more questions. Questions I didn't want to answer.

"Archie, I changed my mind. No cameras. I can't do it. Installing those in our home feels like my freedom is being taken away. Just check all the windows and put an extra dead-lock on each door."

Archie shrugged. "If that's what you want."

I kissed him and rolled over in bed, pulling the covers up to my chin. It wasn't what I wanted. I wanted to live here in peace with my wonderful husband and build a life together. My past had been buried for so many years, why were these reminders showing up now, why not sooner, after I left Listening Lark? Why couldn't I be left in peace?

I should have expected it, of course; nothing stays buried forever. You could never run far enough away, never push the thoughts completely out of your mind, never be free of the events you wished never happened. The past always had a way of sneaking back when you least expected.

I was falling into sleep when another, more terrifying thought popped into my mind. What if it wasn't Brother Jim, but Dream? Real fear snaked through me. The gifts were much more Dream's style; he would play mind games with me. But how could it be him after the way everything ended between us? It was unlikely.

But not impossible.

TWENTY

2023

Aimee

Robin held up a sage green blouse with a scalloped neckline. "What about this? I need some more professional looking tops, especially for meetings with parents and admin."

"I like that a lot. It's a good color on you. I'd get the fuchsia one too. That color would really pop with your dark hair."

She held up the fuchsia top and nodded. "Yeah, this works. Let's look for a dress too. Nothing in black. I have too many dark colors."

"Okay," I said, and we scoured the racks in the women's clothing store. We were on a shopping trip to Elmville's outlet mall; Poplin was too small for any clothing stores, unless you counted bib overalls from the feed store.

"Maybe this?" I held up a white eyelet dress.

"I like it," she said, frowning. "But it's a little too bohemian for me."

I nodded, placing it back on the rack. I used to have a similar dress, years ago. I'd loved it. Its gauzy material fit me just right and it felt light against my skin on hot summer nights. One of my favorite clothing items from the past. Other memories from the past were not so fondly remembered.

Robin examined a deep purple sheath dress. "This?"

I gave her a thumbs up. "Definitely. Love the color."

"Let's go try them on," she said. "Why don't you try the white dress?"

I eyed the clothes rack. "Sure, why not?"

We ended up buying everything and, after a quick stop at the shoe store, we were ready for lunch. A Mexican restaurant close to the outlet mall proved the perfect choice for margaritas and chicken enchiladas.

"So good," I said, eating another bite of enchilada.

"Margaritas are even better," Robin replied, holding up her glass. We clinked our glasses together, although I only had water in mine. I had a bit of a headache and felt alcohol would make it worse. "Cheers!"

"And we got some great clothes." I patted the bag beside me containing the white dress.

Robin took a long drink. "I'm so glad you moved here, Aimee. I have such a good time with you."

"Same," I said. "It's been a long time since I've had a friend to go out with except Archie."

"But that's different. I have a couple of friends I hang out with from time to time, but I don't know, you and I just get along so well, and a lot of them are married and some have kids now. It's just different."

"I agree." I smiled at her. Years ago, I had a friend like Robin. Well, she didn't turn out to be a particularly good friend, but for a time we were inseparable. I liked the closeness, the silliness, in friendship. But sometimes it came at a cost.

"Archie told me about the other night at our annual training yesterday. The light in the attic window?" Robin asked, her brown eyes wide. "So weird."

"Yeah, it was, and Archie thinks it was just moonlight

filtering through the other window, or something," I said flatly. "Or that I imagined it."

Why would he share that information with Robin?

"You two checked the whole house, but didn't find anything?"

"Nothing, and we looked everywhere."

"So scary since they haven't found Angela's killer yet." Robin sighed. "What if that person is still lurking around town? I don't want to scare you, but it's a possibility."

I took another drink. A distinct possibility, indeed. Another possibility was that my presence in Poplin may have brought this person to the town I now called home.

The Commune

Dream

A group of us traveled to a home owned by Raindrop, a notable actress in Hollywood, and a new family member of Listening Lark. The home was in an upscale community known for their lush landscaping, hiking trails, and remote canyons. The house wasn't too far from our current location, but Brother Jim wanted to consider moving Listening Lark to the home because of its size. Raindrop's house had six bedrooms and eight bathrooms, double what we had at Grandmother's house, plus a pool and a guesthouse, all on five acres of land, unheard of in this area. We would have plenty of space for all family members with her house and Grandmother's, and it couldn't have come at a better time. Grandmother's house was becoming increasingly crowded, a good thing in a way because that meant Listening Lark was expanding and growing; but in daily life, I was feeling a bit stressed by the close quarters. I was glad Sunny and I were along for the house tour. We planned to spend the weekend to really get a feel for the space.

The van pulled up to a gated driveway which opened for our entry, and we traveled up the driveway, lush green foliage lining either side until we pulled up to a two-car garage with a wide arched red brick stairway on the side. Bright red geraniums sprouted from terracotta pots, lining the stairway. Another set of stairs sat farther to the right, a large eucalyptus tree and mature vegetation separating them.

Brother Jim parked the van, and we piled out. Sunny grabbed my hand, her eyes bright.

"Let's go explore," she said.

"Please do," Raindrop said, running a hand through her long strawberry blonde mane. "My home is yours. We are family." She grasped Jim Bob's hand and looked at him adoringly. "My family is home."

"So we are. Thank you, Raindrop," Brother Jim said in his usual melodic voice. He turned to us. "Have fun. Pick out a bedroom you would like to spend the weekend. Just not Raindrop's room."

We laughed, and Raindrop moved closer to Brother Jim. They had gotten together immediately after Raindrop arrived at the commune. She was beautiful and rich, an intoxicating combination for Brother Jim.

"Thank you, Brother Jim," Sunny said, her gaze going back to me. "Come on, Dream. Explore with me."

I didn't need a second invitation. I grabbed Sunny's hand, and we ran up the stairs. We reached the front door, wide glass with wood etching, a balcony above, French doors with a half-moon at the top allowing passage to the balcony from inside. The front door opened to a cool spacious foyer with shiny white tile floor. Large, stately potted plants stood on each side of the front door.

We hurried through the archway in the foyer to a large open living room located on the right, done in white and coastal blue with large, deep sectional sofas sitting on a soft rug in various

shades of swirled blue. Another archway led into the cavernous
kitchen, a vision in white and marble with shiny stainless-steel
appliances. A large dining room with a full built-in wall of
shelves displaying china in pristine white, and a large brown
marble-style table in the center of the room. The first floor also
boasted a comfortable study, more built-in shelving, and two
bathrooms, one located in the study, another in the hallway.

Now we moved up the wrought-iron stairway to a bold
patterned hallway, the walls papered with blue and gray in a
loud pattern. The numerous bedrooms, some with balconies
and fireplaces, held soft carpets over hardwood floors, sump-
tuous queen- and king-size beds with bright floral bedspreads
and most had ensuite bathrooms.

Sunny particularly liked the bedroom with an enclosed
balcony that afforded a glimpse of the Pacific Ocean in the
distance. She peered down into the yard below and said in an
excited voice, "Ooh, let's go see the guesthouse by the pool."

We made our way downstairs, out the glass patio doors, to
the yard, first onto a large terracotta patio shaded by lemon
trees. A long, brown wicker table sat in the center; comfortable
cushioned chairs surrounded it. A few lounge chairs to take a
nap in the shade. An archway from the patio led to the pool and
hot tub area, more lemon trees around the space; a wide-open
spot in the vegetation gave a peek of the ocean. To the left of the
pool, tucked away in a cozy grove of orange trees and a huge live
oak, was the guesthouse.

A white adobe structure with a red terracotta roof and large
window planters spilling over with ivy. Sunny ran to open the
door, revealing a small kitchen and living area, more of the
white and coastal blue color scheme, a bedroom, a king-size bed
dominating the space, but still room for a closet and tall dresser,
plus a bathroom with a huge walk-in shower.

Sunny slipped off her sandals and pulled me into the

shower with her, tossing off her tank top and shorts, and turned on the water. I discarded everything I had on.

"Let's make this our new home," she whispered to me, between kisses, her hands rubbing my chest. "We'll call it Sunny Dream."

"Anything you want," I said in a hoarse voice. "This will be our new home."

And it was. For a time.

TWENTY-TWO

2023

Aimee

School started for the year and Archie was busy making lesson plans, getting to know his students and adjusting to a new school. He was very focused on his work and, while I was happy that he got so much enjoyment from it, I did get a bit tired of talking about reading scores and different math strategies, so when the Welcome Back to School Carnival came around, I begged off, claiming a headache. I made my contribution, home-made brownies, to the event. He didn't need me there, and I didn't want to go. I'd leave the socializing to Archie and Robin. The thought of making small talk bored me to tears.

He'd be home late. A group of them were going out for drinks afterward, although Archie probably wouldn't get anything stronger than an iced tea. He wasn't much of a drinker and since he was going out with friends from work, he'd still want to keep it professional.

That meant tonight was all about me. A night to myself, meditation, maybe a little chanting, freeing myself like I used to do. I had missed summer solstice; we were so busy moving and getting the store ready. It was funny, Archie didn't know the strong ties I had to Mother Earth, or the lifestyle I once lived. No, I'd left all of that behind when I left Listening Lark. I wondered if I would ever share this side of myself with him. I also wondered if he hid sides of himself that he didn't want to share with me. Secrecy was an ongoing theme in my relationships. I didn't like talking about my past and didn't see a need to do so, but I think that's unusual. Most people want to share everything about themselves with their significant other, but I viewed it as useless. If you keep digging in the past, you're only looking for trouble in the present.

Lately I'd been feeling old longings for certain aspects of that life. I never could have imagined being married to such a straight arrow like Archie. I was thankful for it though. He grounded me; his practicality and logic were foundations for a happy life. Two people dancing under the sun blissfully unaware, or uncaring, about what happened next, never worked successfully for very long. I'd changed since those days in the sun, but I still had a longing for them. Everything was so strongly felt in that time period at Listening Lark. My sense of touch, sound, sight, and especially emotions. A time when I felt so raw and open to anything, and that anything was possible, even though now with the distance of years gone by, I realized how much of it wasn't a true representation of the time. Many aspects were only illusions of what others wanted me to see, but still, my feelings had never been so vigorous and alive, like a fresh new bud on a flower absorbing all it could grasp.

I sat by the pool, moonlight shimmering off the water, smoking the sacred herb. I didn't smoke often, certainly not as much as I used to, but I kept a stash of it hidden away for special occasions. Maybe I shouldn't say special occasions, just for times when I craved it. Archie didn't know about it. I realized Archie didn't know many of my secrets.

But sometimes you are better off not knowing every single

detail about someone. We all have a past, but some pasts are much more complicated than others. I possessed the complicated type.

I took another drag, my body relaxing into a state I'd been missing. I wore the white bohemian-style dress I'd bought while shopping with Robin last week, its soft cotton material kissing my skin, reminding me of another dress, in another time, barely out of my teens and in love for the first time.

I'd been thinking about Dream quite a bit lately. When I saw him at the farmers' market, the first time we met, I was so drawn to him. Like a moth to a flame, I couldn't stay away from him. I knew we would be together by the frenzy inside of me. I went back to my dorm that night, but Dream consumed my thoughts. He took over all my thoughts and all I wanted was to be with him every minute of the day. Dream. Even his name sounded so delicious to me. A tall, slim guy with dark, almost black, hair that hung wild and loose midway down his back and dark, smoldering eyes that seemed to drink me in as if he'd been traveling in the desert and longed for a glass of cold water. A never-ending thirst. The energy and attraction between us crackled, almost difficult to articulate the sensuality between the two of us. He always said the universe brought us together. I must admit it was a force, a connection between us, unlike anything I experienced in the past.

Irresistible.

But things change.

I sighed, took a long drag, the last of it, and put it into the dirt of a planter on the patio. I stood up, walking across the yard into the cornfield, now with stalks higher than myself. The long leaves brushed against my bare arms as I walked through the tight narrow rows. A full moon shone above me, majestic in its beauty, and I raised my hands to the moon goddess shining her light down on my mortal body.

I tilted my head back, itchy leaves of the corn scratching my arms as I walked farther into the field, its claustrophobic environment securing me in a tight cocoon. My bare feet traveled lightly; my toes dug into the dusty earth beneath me. Mother Earth's life-giving soil, while the moon goddess bathed me in her brilliant white light.

I stopped and drank in the energy pulsating through my body. My mind flickered with memories, some good, some not, but in this moment of enlightenment I could feel Dream's hands on me, traveling the curves and sweet spots of my body. I could smell his scent and felt his lips on mine, reliving the memories of so long ago. The sacred herb and the moon energy played with my rational mind, and I'm not sure how long I stayed in that trancelike state.

Then I heard Archie calling for me, almost as if he stood at the end of a tunnel. I snapped out of my dazed state and ran toward his voice, dodging through the cornstalks scratching me and snagging my dress once, then the field cleared and I entered the yard, running, my white dress flowing behind me, a vision I'm sure under the bright harvest moon.

"What..." Archie stared at me. "What are you doing?"

I said nothing. Instead, I gave him a long, slow kiss, savoring the taste of his mouth and the feel of his body touching my own. He responded and we tumbled onto the soft grass, our bodies intertwined.

His hands were on me now, lovingly caressing my body, seeking what lay beneath the thin cotton material of my dress. We quickly discarded our clothes, bathing only in moonlight from the moon goddess, writhing on the cool grass, seeking the pleasure we both craved. A thought filtered into my mind as we rose to climax.

I wondered if Dream watched from afar.

TWENTY-THREE

2023

Aimee

The morning at the store passed quickly. I'd begun adding products of local farms to my merchandise such as goat's milk hand lotion, alpaca scarves and hats, homemade yogurt, various planters, including fresh herbs, perfect to fit into a kitchen window ledge, homemade sourdough bread, and homemade candies. My little market was filling its shelves and all the products were selling nicely. The neighboring farms were happy to have a central place in town to sell their wares, in addition to their small in-house farm stands.

I hired a part-time employee, a young Amish woman, to work a few hours a week. Rachel lived on a dairy farm on the outskirts of town and usually walked to work, although sometimes her brother, Eli, would drop her off in the horse and buggy. She was a quiet eighteen-year-old with bright eyes, and a hard worker. The dark solemn Amish uniform did little to enhance anyone's looks, but Rachel's beauty was evident even with the constant oppressive black and rigidly pulled back hair, covered in a black cap. I would think Amish women would have a splitting headache from having their hair so tightly pinned up all day. I certainly couldn't stand it.

I put the last bottle of goat's milk lotion on the shelf and arranged the sourdough loaves next to the homemade jams. Everything was ready to open tomorrow—time to close for today. I already called Poplin Chicken for takeout to pick up on the way home for dinner. I went to lock the door.

John stood outside.

I opened the door. "Oh, hey, John. I was just locking up for the day,"

"I just wanted to get some more of that strawberry jam. Grandma loves it on her toast in the morning and she ate the last of it this morning," he replied.

"Um, okay, sure," I said, letting him inside. I walked over to the jam. "How many would you like?"

"Give me three," he said. "That should last a while."

"Sure." I took the three jars to the counter and rang them up.

"I want to ask you something," he said, swiping his debit card for the purchase.

"Okay," I said, hesitant.

"Is Robin angry at me?"

I slowly placed the jam jars into a paper bag, wishing I could ignore the question. *Why is he asking me?*

"Um... I don't think so," I replied, handing him the bag.

He took the bag but didn't move. "It's seeming like she's avoiding me."

I frowned. I didn't want to have this conversation with him. What was I supposed to say? She's not interested in you because you're a boring guy. Bordering creepy.

"Well, it's the beginning of the school year," I said breezily. "Always a busy time. Archie barely has time for me."

John leaned closer to me and smiled. "Well, I know that's not true. Archie always has time for you."

A perfect example. John's words were fine. Nothing wrong with the statement, but the way he said it gave me a chill up my spine. He made my skin crawl.

"That's the only thing I can think of," I replied briskly. "Now, I must close up. I have a takeout order to pick up."

John met my gaze. "I'll be seeing you." He walked out of the store.

I locked the door and watched him walk down the street.

I signed in with the front office, chatted a bit with the school secretary, then took my large container of chocolate chip cookies and walked down the hall to Archie's classroom. The hallway was filled with brightly colored drawings with detailed writings of 'What I Did This Summer' by numerous students. I read a few, some very neat, some messy, but all had similar themes. They went to the beach, to the amusement park, the mountains, the pool. I continued to Archie's area; his room was halfway down the hallway. I opened the door to see Archie sitting at his desk in the back of the room, eating a sandwich. Robin sat on the edge of his desk, facing him, eating from a bag of potato chips, her long, tanned legs dangling down.

"Hey, Aimee," she greeted in a friendly tone, scooting off Archie's desk.

"Hey," I said, wondering why she was sitting on my husband's desk in the first place.

"Babe, I thought you were stopping in later. Who's at the store?" Archie asked.

"Rachel's there," I said, setting the container of cookies on his desk. "Here are the cookies for the bake sale."

"Great, thanks for making those." He smiled. "You're my secret weapon; we're competing against Robin's class to see who raises the most money from the sale. The winning class gets an ice cream party."

"Oh, fun," I remarked, pausing to admire my handsome husband. With his dark blond hair and warm brown eyes, he was the opposite of Dream in every way. Reliable, practical, what was that old saying? Had his head on straight. Yes. You wouldn't catch Archie clad in white, chanting in the early morning hours or losing several days to a sacred herb celebration. No, Archie had his mind on reading scores and bake sales.

Did he also have his eye on Robin?

The thought darted out of nowhere. I stood there silent as Robin babbled on about the cheesecake brownies she was making for the bake sale, her long chestnut brown hair brushing the top of her slim shoulders. She wore the deep purple sheath dress we bought earlier at the outlet mall, and it fit her well. Her flawless skin, even under the harsh fluorescent lighting of the classroom, gave off a dewy glow. She was very pretty.

I brushed the thought away. I'd obsessed over these same things in the past and the outcome was never good. Archie and Robin were friendly colleagues, that's all, and she was my friend. I wouldn't allow my imagination to take hold. I'd only focus on the facts as they presented themselves. Besides, Archie was devoted to me, I knew that.

Archie held up half his turkey sandwich. "Want some?"

I declined, but I snagged the bag of grapes lying on his desk. "No, but I'll take these."

Robin glanced at the clock. "Ten minutes until our students are back from lunch. I want to pick up some books from the library, so I better get going. See you, Aimee," she said, sailing out of the room.

I popped a grape into my mouth and turned my attention to Archie. "You two are getting close."

He laughed awkwardly. "Close? I don't know about that. We work well together. She's a good partner teacher."

I nodded and ate another grape.

TWENTY-FOUR

2023

Aimee

My head, heavy as lead, lay cushioned on the soft bedroom pillow. I was awake, but kept my eyes shut, exhausted even after a full night's sleep. I rolled over in bed and slowly lifted my eyes. Nine fifteen, according to the clock on the nightstand. Thankfully, it was Monday, and I had no plans today. The store was closed on Mondays. If I wanted to stay in bed all day, I could, which at this point seemed like a distinct possibility.

I felt hungover, but none of my activity the night before would warrant such a feeling. We ate dinner—baked chicken, rice, and green beans—and later had a slice of apple pie with a cup of tea. No alcohol. No sacred herb. But this morning I felt as if I'd been partying until the wee hours of the night. I buried my head in the pillow. Maybe I was getting sick.

I stayed that way for several minutes. I didn't feel like getting out of my warm cocoon, but even if I could take it easy today, I still needed to feed the chickens and the rabbits we just bought. Finally, I dragged myself out of bed and stumbled into the bathroom. I splashed cold water on my face and brushed my teeth, getting rid of my strong morning breath. I went back into our bedroom and debated getting dressed or just leaving on my pajamas, a cute shorts and tank set in a rosy pink color. I decided on the pajamas, but grabbed my white cotton robe from the bathroom. I needed coffee. Desperately.

I walked downstairs. Usually I made a K-Cup if I was the only one home, but today I needed a whole pot. I got the coffee going, the aroma already perking me up, and noticed a note on the kitchen island.

You look so beautiful when you are asleep. Xo

I recognized Archie's handwriting. Although I was fairly certain it was from him, still a little fizzle of doubt ran through me. I grabbed my phone.

> Thanks for the sweet note. Xo

No response. He was probably teaching his class. Ten minutes passed.

A text popped up from him.

> You do look beautiful when you sleep. You always look beautiful.

Relief spread through me. Yes, the note was from Archie. I sent a heart emoji in response to his text and rummaged around in the cabinets to locate the largest coffee cup I could find. I filled it, leaving room to add creamer, and took a long sip of the hot delight. Ahh... caffeine.

I sat at the kitchen table, sipping my coffee, hoping it would wake up my slow-moving body. The house remained silent, aside from the tick tock of the kitchen clock. The comfortable silence was welcome to me. Not the eerie silence of another person lurking, hiding in its cover, waiting to make their next move. No, this morning was the peaceful silence of a secure home.

My thoughts focused on breakfast. I didn't feel like making eggs, but a piece of toast with my homemade strawberry jam sounded delicious to me, so I went about making it.

As I buttered the toast and spread the jam my thoughts traveled back to yesterday in Archie's classroom. Maybe I had overreacted with my suspicions about Robin. I'd done it in the past. Neither had given me any reason to distrust them. And Robin was a good friend.

I took a bite of toast and drank my second cup of coffee. I was waking up now and feeling better, finally. I glanced at the clock and finished off the coffee. I had to feed and water the chickens. They'd be looking for me by now.

Slipping on my flip-flops by the door, I walked outside. It was mid-September now, still warm, but there was a nip in the morning air, enough to let you know autumn was around the corner.

The chickens were waiting for me, squawking, and stamping around in their enclosed yard. I gave them a scoop of chicken feed and filled their water dispenser. I gathered the eggs, washed and dried them with a paper towel, put them into egg cartons, then deposited them into the barn refrigerator. I wished now that I had gotten dressed before heading to the barn. This clothing would be going straight into the washer.

By now it was probably close to eleven and our mail likely sat in the mailbox at the end of the lane, usually arriving around nine thirty or ten. I tightened the sash on my robe and walked down our paved lane.

The warm sunny day brightened my body and mind, a welcome departure from my sluggish entry to the day. My flip-flops clicked on the blacktop, and I soon arrived at the mailbox. I opened it, took out the stack of mail, and walked back to the house, flipping through the envelopes.

A few pieces of junk mail, two magazines, a bill from our insurance company, and a yellow card envelope with no return address. The addressee, on a typed computer label, stopped me midway up the lane.

Sunshine Lotus.

I quickly tore open the envelope. Inside was a photograph of myself and Dream. We stood in front of the guesthouse, at Raindrop's house, our home at the time. I wore a pale-yellow bikini; he wore blue swimming trunks with a white stripe down the side. Swimming suits were pretty much all we wore that year, sometimes not even those. Dream's arm was draped around my waist and mine around his. We smiled at the camera, or whoever took the picture. I remembered that day. I remembered who took the picture.

Brother Jim. Or Jim Bob as Dream sometimes called him, much to Brother Jim's annoyance, if any other family members were around.

I clutched the picture and ran up the lane, back into our house, locking the door behind me.

The Commune
Dream

The Zen Yoga Deck at Raindrop's house was a pleasure I never knew I needed. Located through the orange and lemon trees, behind the pool, in a grove of coastal live oaks and sycamore trees, was a large bamboo platform with a thatched roof and sheer white curtains on every side that flowed beautifully in a soft breeze.

Sunny and I were there that morning, just past sunrise, with our purple yoga mats stretched out on the platform, wispy curtains blowing in the early morning breeze. It was a bit cool at that time of day but invigorating. Raindrop and River joined us that morning. We were all nude.

Nude yoga is such a freeing experience. Not necessarily sexual, but certainly sexy. No, the practice is more about baring yourself physically and mentally, removing anything which could hinder you from a higher consciousness, one with Mother Nature, the mind, body, and soul. Without any physical barriers, your body in its natural state is more open to receiving the positive energy you seek. This was an experience I was certain everyone could enjoy in their lives.

We were in Cat-Cow flow, oxygen filling my body with each breath. I stared at Sunny, beside me, her tight, tanned body a feast for my eyes. I couldn't think of any place I'd rather be in that moment in time.

The air hung sweet, the scent of fresh cut grass still evident from River's yardwork yesterday, mingling with the aromatic purple sage that grew around the yoga deck, mixed with lush green maidenhair ferns. We completed our last Cat-Cow and moved into Savasana. As we lingered in the restorative pose, I listened to birds twittering in the trees around the space, bidding their good morning to all. I breathed deeply, exhaling away any lingering stress that may have resided in my body. A deep calm filled my body.

Sunny reached for my hand, and I stood and lifted her from the mat. River and Raindrop did the same, all of us in a calm, relaxed state. I allowed my gaze to drift to Raindrop for a moment while Sunny picked up her yoga mat. She'd had breast implants done not too long ago and I must say, they were very well done. My gaze did not linger though; I knew better than that. Sunny had a jealous streak, and her sweetness could turn to venom in a flash.

River caught my stealth look and smiled. "Beautiful out here, isn't it," he remarked.

I nodded and grinned. Sunny and I waved goodbye to them and headed back to the guesthouse. Before we went inside, we took a quick dip in the pool. A few minutes later, Raindrop and River ran past the pool, laughing, and chasing each other. They disappeared into the house.

"Do you think they're having sex?" I asked Sunny. She leaned against the steps in the pool.

"Yes. Definitely," she replied, running a hand through her

long golden hair. "I heard them the other night, out here in the pool. You were sleeping."

"Oh, really," I asked. "Did you watch?"

She flicked water at me. "I'll never tell."

I laughed and swam the length of the pool. Raindrop was one of Brother Jim's women. As far as most of the family knew, he was with Raindrop and Moonbeam. He spent his time between Grandmother's house, where Moonbeam lived, and here because of the growing tension between the two women. His assistant, Jasmine, traveled with him to both locations. She often joined both relationships.

Oh, Jim Bob was going to flip when he found out about River. For all his talk about sexual freedom, he expected to be the only one for his chosen ladies. The old double standard.

Well, maybe that's one thing we had in common.

TWENTY-SIX

2023

Aimee

I placed the photograph and the envelope on the kitchen island and stared at both. My skin prickled, my forehead slick with sweat as I studied the photo. I was sick of this person playing games. I wanted them to come out and tell me clearly what they wanted. Were they having fun, thinking they were scaring me? Although today, looking at this photograph only brought back good memories for me. Happy times.

The idyllic months living in Raindrop's guesthouse cast feelings of freedom and love in my heart and mind. I couldn't take my eyes off the photo. Dream and I were so happy, smiling by Raindrop's pool. My heart ached looking at him, feeling such sadness at how everything used to be between us. It was a time when I thought anything was possible. Listening Lark was the first place I felt like I truly belonged and was loved. Where I was part of something bigger than myself and the longing inside me was finally satisfied. There, I hadn't been lonely anymore. Tears welled in my eyes as I continued to stare at the picture. I

missed all of them. Raindrop. River. Even Moonbeam, but especially Dream. If I could have stayed in a time loop in Listening
Lark during the good times, I would in a heartbeat. I would have
never left. Chanting in the mountains. The tiny cabin Dream
and I shared when I first moved in. The guesthouse at Raindrop's house. Big dinners together. They were my family.
Listening Lark was a utopia.

Until it wasn't.

I snapped out of my daydream, wiped my tears and thought
logically about the photo, leaving the sentiment behind, where
it should be left. Why send this to me now? After so many
years? Time passed and people moved on. I didn't even know if
Listening Lark still existed. I didn't want to know. I wouldn't
live in the past, but I needed to figure out what they wanted
from me. What was the goal of these random gifts, if I would
call them so, and strange occurrences at our house? To scare
me? To hurt Archie and I?

One thing I knew.

Archie could not know about my past. I had closed the door
on that part of my life and I would never open it again.

And if this person thought they would scare me with a few
well-placed objects and lights turning on and off they had
forgotten who I was, or maybe they never really knew me.
Sometimes I wondered if anyone truly knew me.

Having people underestimate you is most often a gift.

It gives you an advantage. At least in my experience.

I glanced at the photo one last time before putting it away,
and another thought crossed my mind.

This might be Dream's way of saying he forgave me.

Could I forgive him?

What if Listening Lark was calling me home?

· · ·

I rummaged through my closet trying to locate the shoebox of memories from my time at the commune. My time with Dream. I shoved a pile of purses to the side, sure I'd put the box underneath, but there was nothing.

I sat back on the hardwood floor. We only moved in a few months ago, and I remembered placing it under the purses. Why I even kept it, I didn't know, but I couldn't throw it out. Those things in that box were the only physical reminders of that period of my life. I dug around in my closet a little more, but it was useless. The box was gone.

Whoever sent me the photo and put the turquoise necklace on the vanity took the entire box. I remembered all the contents of the box. Necklace, a few photos, two dried lotus flowers, a soft T-shirt of Dream's and a key to the guesthouse.

Raindrop gave me the key one afternoon when Dream and River went to pick up Brother Jim from the other house. I was sunning in a lounge chair by the pool and she walked outside, directly to me, clothed in a silky pink robe, looking gorgeous as always, and pressed the key into my hand.

"It's the guesthouse key," she said in a low tone.

"Uh... we don't lock the doors." I shook my head. "I don't need this."

"Keep it," she said, glancing around. Nobody was in our immediate area. "I have a key to my bedroom. Sometimes I lock my bedroom door when I'm avoiding Brother Jim. I don't need to come into my bedroom in my house and find him waiting for me."

"You do?" I said, shocked.

Raindrop looked at me. "He's been changing lately, been more physically aggressive. He's different than I originally thought, all of this is. I'm not putting up with that. And he's related to Dream, so maybe they share that tendency."

"No," I said firmly. "Dream is not like that."

"Take the key," she said. "You might need it one day."

So, I took it.

Raindrop was right.

I did use it.

TWENTY-SEVEN

2023

Aimee

"Okay, third grade, today we are going to talk about good nutrition!" Robin said in a sing-song voice. She clapped her hands and the students clapped with her. "Can anyone name some healthy foods?"

A blond boy in the front of the room raised his hands. "Apples! I like to eat apples with peanut butter, but not in school because you are allergic."

"Yes! Thank you, Conner," Robin said. "You like apples with peanut butter. I like apples, but no peanut butter because Miss Kent is allergic to peanut butter. Anyone else? Yes, Ally." She pointed to a dark-haired girl in the back of the class.

"Tomatoes! Bananas! Carrots!" shouted Ally.

"Yes! Yes! Yes! All healthy foods," Robin agreed. "And today a friend of mine is visiting our class. Everyone say hello to Mrs. Greencastle. She is married to Mr. Greencastle, who teaches the other third grade, and she's here today to talk to us about healthy foods."

"Hello, Mrs. Greencastle," the students greeted in unison.

I waved.

"Mrs. Greencastle owns a store right here in Poplin." Robin widened her eyes.

"Poplin Fresh!" Ally shouted.

Robin pointed at her. "Yes, but don't call out. Guess what Mrs. Greencastle sells in her store? No call outs. I want to see hands raised."

Small hands flew up around the classroom. Robin chose a girl with pigtails from the center of the class. "Zoey."

"Food," Zoey said hesitantly.

"Yes, food," said Robin. "What kind of food? Let's say it together."

"Healthy food!" The classroom vibrated with voices.

Robin motioned me over to the center front of the room. I smiled at the children.

"That's right, I sell healthy food at my store, Poplin Fresh We sell some of the foods you mentioned today. Tomatoes, apples, carrots, and so many more delicious and healthy foods," I began. "Eating healthy foods is so important to keeping your body healthy."

I went through my presentation and concluded by giving each student a snack of an apple, fresh-baked blueberry muffin, and apple cider. The students were delighted with my surprise snack. Robin was happy the snack kept them busy for a short time.

"Thank you so much for doing this," Robin said, taking a bite of muffin, leaning against her desk.

"Sure, no problem. It was fun," I replied. "I'm presenting in Archie's class tomorrow afternoon."

"Yeah, he's a day or two behind me in the lesson," remarked Robin.

She looked at me. "So how are things with you? I feel like I haven't talked to you much since the start of school. It's always so crazy in the beginning."

"Um... not much," I said. I certainly wasn't going to tell her about everything going on at home, although Archie shared the attic scare with her. No way would I tell her about the photo. I liked Robin, but not that much. I hadn't even shared it with Archie. How could I if I didn't want him to know about my past? He thought I was a local Philly girl that worked in a coffee shop and lived with her elderly aunt. He knew the basics about me, but I didn't want him to know the rest.

"Oh, John was asking about you the other day in the store. He wanted to know if you were mad at him."

Robin frowned. "Ugh, what are we, fourteen? Checking with my friend to see if I'm mad at him. I would think he'd get the hint by now. I don't want to go out with him!"

"Maybe you should tell him that directly. He doesn't seem like a guy who picks up on obvious clues. Just tell him exactly what you just said to me," I replied.

"Maybe, but I don't think that will work either."

"Why?"

Robin lowered her voice. "He used to be interested in Margie who works at Poplin Chicken. She didn't go out with him at all and flat out said she wasn't interested. He got a little stalkerish. Hanging around her work, surprise visits to her house. Nothing sinister, but uncomfortable. She told me this after she heard we went on a date."

"Really?" I asked. Not particularly surprised though.

"Yeah, he only stopped when Margie started dating a cop. They just got engaged."

I snorted. "Then we just need to find you a sexy cop."

"Yes, please." Robin laughed.

Archie tossed the newspaper on the kitchen table. The *Poplin Times* was still publishing a Sunday paper edition. The daily paper was available only online, but Sundays you had a choice of either. I rather looked forward to a paper to read on Sundays.

"Read the cover story," he said. "It's about Angela."

"Oh." I grabbed the paper and read the article.

The search for Angela's killer continued. Several leads were being investigated, but nothing substantial had been discovered. A forty-thousand-dollar reward, increased yesterday, was now being offered for any information leading to the arrest of the perpetrator.

"So, I guess the theory about the married man she was seeing fell through," I remarked.

"I guess so," said Archie. "I hope they find this person soon."

"Yeah, me too." Worry filtered through me, snaking its grip throughout my body.

"I know the lights in the attic scared you, but I don't think it's anything to worry about," he commented. "I want you to feel safe in our own home. I'm sure it had to be the moonlight filtering through the other window."

"Sure," I agreed, even though I did *not* agree with his statement.

Did all my unexpected surprises lead to Angela's killer? I didn't know what the connection would be if this was true. Instead, all these occurrences held a distinctive personal tone directed squarely at me. Listening Lark was haunting me.

I know where you are.

I know what you did.

"What do you think?" Archie's voice broke into my thoughts.

"What?" I asked. I placed the paper on the table.

"Do you care if John comes over for dinner next Saturday? I'll cook."

I stared at him. "Why?"

"Because I want to have him over. To say thanks for taking care of our fields. Because we're friends," he said.

"Are we? And we pay him for the fields."

"Yes, I like him; why is this a big deal?" he asked, walking over to the refrigerator. He got the orange juice out and set it on the counter, then selected a glass from the cupboard, and poured the juice. "Why do you have such a problem with John?"

I sighed. "Fine, we'll have him over."

"You really don't like him?"

"I don't really know him."

"Do you want to?"

I smiled at him. "If you want me to get to know him, I will."

Archie smiled, drained the juice, and walked over to me. He bent down to kiss me.

"That's all I want. I want to make friends here. Real friends, community."

I nodded. "I know, so do I."

"Seems like you and Robin are getting closer," he remarked.

"We are. She is probably my favorite person here," I said, grinning at him. "Besides you."

He stared at me as he does sometimes, as if I'm the most beautiful woman in the world.

Same as Dream used to do so many years ago.

Dammit, I didn't want to think about him.

Was it strange Archie and I didn't have any family or friends? Yes, odd. I know why I didn't, but Archie, friendly, gregarious Archie, didn't have a best friend from high school or a close college roommate? Well, that wasn't completely true. He had a childhood friend, Nick, who lived in Oregon, but I never met him, had never even seen a picture of him. I spoke to him a couple times when Archie talked to him on the phone, but they never video chatted, only phone calls and text messages. I always thought it was a sign that Archie and I were meant for one another. We needed each other.

We made each other whole.

I hadn't felt whole in a long time. I wondered if I ever had.

Crispness circulated in the air this clear, sunny September morning. I pulled out of our lane and turned right, heading into town. A pickup truck passed me; an older man wearing a baseball cap waved to me. I waved back and smiled. This was something I had become used to since we'd moved here. Everybody waved to everyone they passed on the road, whether you knew them, or not. A nice sentiment, but it became tiresome at times. Sometimes I just wanted to drive and be invisible, lost in my own little world.

I glanced in my rearview mirror at the dark sedan behind me, a bit too close. I sped up, but they continued to clip along, keeping pace with me. Were they following me? I struggled to see the driver, but the windows were tinted, so I didn't have much luck.

I slowed down, moving at a snail's pace. The driver was really tailgating me now but when a passing lane opened up, he flew around me, blowing his horn in irritation. That was okay with me. At least I knew he wasn't following me. And I guess my theory about everyone waving in this town would have a few outliers. Slowly, my heart rate returned to normal.

I turned on some music and drove the short distance to the store. My phone rang. Robin. I clicked answer on my dashboard.

"Hey, girl," I said.

"Hey," she said. "What are you doing?"

"Driving to the store. What about you?"

"Stuffing students' take-home folders." She sighed. "I have ten minutes until the bell rings and they start rolling in. I wanted to ask you something."

"Yes?"

"I won the couple massage gift card at a spa in Elmville on Back-to-School Night. Do you want to go with me?"

"Yes, I do! When?"

"This Saturday?"

"Okay, in the afternoon? I'm in the store in the morning."

"Great, see you then."

I disconnected the call. I hadn't had a massage in years. Right now, it sounded heavenly.

We lay face down on the massage table, our bodies calm and relaxed after a deep tissue massage and enjoying the hot towels lying atop us. Soothing music played, lights dimmed, and eucalyptus scent filled the room. I could have easily fallen asleep.

"So amazing," I said. "Thanks for inviting me."

"So glad you came," Robin murmured. "This feels amazing."

We relaxed in silence for a few minutes.

"Did you see that masseur out at the reception area?" I asked.

"Mmm... the guy, yeah."

"He was cute. You should ask him out."

She laughed. "Yeah, right."

"Seriously."

"Maybe, he is cute."

We stayed there for a few more minutes, then put on the white plush robes. Next was lunch in the spa café. Everyone wore their robes in the café. Relaxing music filled the space. I could have gotten used to that kind of relaxation.

"Oh, I needed this." Robin pierced the romaine lettuce of her grilled chicken salad, same as me. "The first weeks of school are so exhausting."

I nodded. "Yeah, Archie's wiped out too. Well, you not only

have class; it's all the meetings and after school paperwork that adds up."

"True, but I love it," Robin said. "I love helping children learn and grow. It's so rewarding to me."

"I imagine so," I remarked.

"I can't wait until I have my own kids," she said, smiling. "I've always wanted to be a mother."

"Really?"

One topic that gave me hesitancy was motherhood. I didn't know if I wanted to have children. Archie and I had pushed the subject to the side. We didn't want kids now, we knew that and maybe our feelings would change, but until then, we were fine with it being just us. The thought of being responsible for another human being scared me. I didn't know if I possessed the abilities to handle it, or if I wanted the task.

"What about you and Archie?" Robin asked. "When do you want to have kids? Oh, he'll be such a good dad."

I looked at her. Funny how she left me out of that statement.

She picked up on her slip.

"You'll be a great mother, of course!"

Of course I will. I stabbed my romaine lettuce and shoved it into my mouth.

TWENTY-EIGHT
2016

The Commune
Dream

Raindrop's property wasn't far from hiking trails and outstanding vistas in the Santa Monica Mountains, which boasted some spectacular lookouts and dramatic deep canyons, we frequently visited. Today we planned a sunrise chant at a stunning spot with panoramic views of the canyons. All our family perched on large, red rocks, our hands raised as we swayed and chanted, welcoming the burgeoning oranges and yellows of the glorious sunrise given to us by Mother Earth. Sunny and I sat toward the back. She didn't like heights.

Brother Jim sat on the center rock dressed in a white gown with gold embroidery around the wide V-neck. We were all dressed in similar garb, men and women, a sea of white flowing gowns with golden highlights. Moonbeam and Lilac made each garment with love for their fellow brothers and sisters. The gowns were knee-length to allow for hiking up the sometimes difficult trails. We all wore sturdy hiking sandals.

"Brothers and sisters, we gather at this beacon of nature's

beauty to celebrate our life, our freedom, and bringing our manifestations to reality!" Brother Jim stood up, lifting his arms; swaths of white fabric hung like wings on him as he lifted his arms. The imagery of him against a dramatic morning sky was impressive, even to me. I knew how far Jim Bob was from being an angel.

"Our work here at Listening Lark has only just begun. Brothers and sisters, we must cling to one another, open ourselves up to new experiences in order to maintain our current utopia and higher understanding." Brother Jim paused for effect. "We are all one in this family. One beating heart that is Listening Lark!"

He signaled to River, who began playing his guitar, and Branch, who played the bongo drum. The family raised their arms high and fell into a familiar chant. Brother Jim swayed on the rock, arms raised, white gown swaying, obviously enjoying the hum of his flock.

My arms were raised too. I liked the unity of Listening Lark. I embraced it even if I knew Jim Bob was a con man. I chose to ignore that fact, and his secrets, just as he ignored my secrets. Maybe that made me no better than Jim Bob.

Afterward, we broke up into smaller groups. Some brought picnic baskets with food and had a bite to eat; some members explored the numerous hiking trails. Sunny and I joined Jim Bob and Raindrop on a nearby trail.

"What a great morning for a hike," Brother Jim exclaimed.

"A bit early for me," Raindrop grumbled.

Brother Jim glared at her.

Things between them had gotten tense over the last few weeks, and in any other relationship Jim Bob would be done with her, but he needed Raindrop's wealth; it made his life, and all of our lives, better, so he'd give more effort, hopefully. I certainly didn't want to move out of the guesthouse.

"I really enjoyed your talk this morning," Sunny chimed in. "So inspiring."

Brother Jim smiled. "Thank you, Sunny. There's something special about chanting in the mountains that bonds us as a family."

Sunny nodded, and we walked along the trail at a leisurely pace, chatting with each other as we moved along. Sunny and I stopped to admire some deep purple flowers while Jim Bob and Raindrop moved ahead. They were a distance ahead of us when we resumed walking, but still visible. And I realized that they were arguing.

Sunny and I stared in shock as we watched Jim Bob suddenly slap Raindrop across the face and grab her arm.

"What's he doing?" Sunny asked, moving forward. "We have to help her."

I pulled her back. "No, don't interfere."

"He's hitting her. We have to do something." Sunny struggled to get away from my grasp, breaking free and giving me a disgusted look. "I'm going to help her."

"No!" I hissed. I pushed her back against a tree, hard. Too hard.

She brushed against a sharp tree branch on the right side and it sliced her cheek. Blood appeared, running down her face.

"Dream!" she yelled, touching the wound. She pushed me away.

"I'm so sorry," I said, feeling terrible. "I didn't mean to do that."

Raindrop ran past us. Jim Bob was nowhere to be seen. Sunny went around me and ran after Raindrop.

I was alone in the woods.

I hoped Sunny wouldn't be mad at me tomorrow. Now she slept peacefully in our bed, antibiotic ointment and a bandage protecting her cut. She was angry at me when she fell asleep and I couldn't blame her.

I didn't want to interfere with Jim Bob's personal relationships; I knew that would only enrage him. I couldn't risk angering him. My secrets were worse than his and he knew it.

He had helped me bury them.

I shouldn't have gotten rough with Sunny today. I had just wanted her to stop. Stop! She didn't know how precarious my relationship was with Jim Bob. He and I promised to never turn on one another. Any secrets we knew about each other would go to the grave.

I looked at Sunny in blissful slumber and remembered another woman from years ago. She too had long blonde hair, although a bit darker in color than Sunny's.

I remembered her lifeless body lying in bed.

TWENTY-NINE

2023

Aimee

Later, on Saturday evening, the dining room was warm and cozy from the lit fireplace, a simple brick structure with a long walnut mantle above, displaying some of Aunt Lou's favorite pottery pieces in bright blues and yellows. A creamy butter yellow tablecloth covered the oval walnut table, and a blue vase filled with fresh flowers from my garden, probably the last of the season, sat in the center of the table. Aunt Lou's dark blue bone china, joined by her Depression water glasses, displayed at three place settings.

Archie had originally planned to grill and eat outside on the patio, but the day turned out cool and rainy, so we decided to make roast chicken, parmesan potatoes, and green beans and eat in the dining room. Chocolate cake with peanut butter icing for dessert. It was nice setting up the dining room, even if it was to host John Larabe.

I stared at Aunt Lou's pottery on the mantle. She had been a talented artist in her younger years, although her money didn't come from her time as an artist, but rather her third husband, who she always said was her favorite person in the world. Like my Archie.

She was a kind woman, and I was thankful for the care she gave me when I needed it. At the end, when I found her crumpled at the bottom of her stairs in the upscale Society Hill home that she shared with me, it was her time to go. She was frail, suffering from memory issues, and becoming increasingly dependent on me. I'd hired a daily nurse to come in to help her a few days a week, but she was unreliable, and Aunt Lou would soon have needed more care. Though it had hurt to lose my final blood relative, her fall down the stairs had been a blessing in some ways. Funny how endings were often the gateways to new beginnings.

I walked into the kitchen where Archie was checking on the roast chicken in the oven.

"How's it looking?" I asked.

"Good. Fifteen minutes and it's done," he said. "Perfect timing because John should be here soon."

"Great," I replied, tidying the kitchen sink and loading the dishwasher.

"He's going to be disappointed you didn't invite Robin," Archie remarked, looking at me.

"She wouldn't have come. Why do you not get that she's not interested in spending time with him?" I asked. "Or do you want to spend more time with her?"

"What?" He frowned. "No, of course not. Forget I said anything."

"Done," I said, heading back to the dining room.

"This chicken is delicious, Aimee," John remarked, taking a second helping from the serving plate in the center of the table.

"Good, Archie made dinner. I made the cake last night. Team effort," I replied.

"Well, everything tastes great," said John, smiling.

"We're glad you're enjoying it," Archie said. "And glad you could come over tonight."

"I don't turn down many dinner invitations, probably because I don't get many." John laughed. "But, I have to admit, I was hoping Robin would be here."

Archie shot me a look from across the table. "Maybe next time," he said.

I smiled, pierced a small potato, covered in parmesan cheese and garlic, and popped it into my mouth. Doubtful. Robin was right, we were going to have to either find her a boyfriend or fabricate one to get rid of this guy. He could not take a hint, or even several hints.

"So, how do you like living in Poplin?" John asked.

"I'm really enjoying it," I said. "I love having all the space, and raising fresh food has always been important to me. Nothing like going out to your backyard, picking a bunch of apples and making a pie."

"Even if the attic lights freak you out a bit." Archie laughed.

I glared at him. "Well, we figured that out."

I bristled, irritated by his comment. Why would he bring that up around John? Just like he shared it with Robin earlier. If we had an issue at our house, it should stay with us, not be shared with others. Why was he being such a smart-ass? I didn't know why he found it so funny. He wouldn't if he knew who was doing it. He would be completely freaked out if anyone from Listening Lark confronted him, especially if it was who I suspected.

"Oh, if you're having electrical issues, I can look at it," said John, taking a sip of water from Aunt Lou's blue goblet. "I'm pretty good with electrical work."

"Good to know, thanks," replied Archie, his gaze meeting mine. "We're okay now, but I'll let you know if something comes up."

"Yes, thanks, John," I said, smiling. *Like hell you're hanging around my attic doing electrical work.* I raised my blue goblet and took a long drink. "It'll be good to have a friend who's so handy with home repairs."

A look of relief flashed across Archie's face. "Definitely. So, John, still have room for chocolate cake with peanut butter icing? And ice cream?"

"Sure," he replied. "Well, that's a treat we wouldn't be having if Robin was here. Not with her peanut allergy."

Archie and I both nodded.

"That's right," I replied, standing up. "You know a lot about Robin."

"I guess so." John smiled, directed at me, his eyes seemingly friendly, but I could feel something else lurking behind those dark eyes.

THIRTY

2023

Aimee

"Girls' night!" Robin exclaimed, walking into the spacious family room with two large bottles of sangria.

"Yeah!" I agreed, holding up my wine glass. "Fill it up!"

I was spending the night at Robin's house. A fun girls-in Saturday night. She lived with her parents, but they left that morning for a three-week trip out west. She wanted to have a wine and movie night. Sleeping over made sense if I was drinking wine. Archie was on his own tonight. He was going out for pizza with John. Of course he was.

"I wish Caitlin could have made it," she said, pouring the wine. "You'd really like her, but she has a new baby, and the sweet boy consumes her time, understandably so."

I nodded. "I'm sure I'll meet her one day."

Robin flopped on the large, dark leather sectional next to me and clicked on Netflix. She scrolled until a creepy thriller caught our attention.

"Creepy, but not gory," she said, digging her hand into the

bowl of popcorn sitting on the wide coffee table in front of us. "That's the kind of movie I like."

"Agreed," I said, sipping my wine.

The movie was short, but effectively scary, in a psychological sense.

"Should we call for a pizza?" she asked.

"Do they deliver out here?" I asked. That was something I had to get used to living out in the country. No food delivery.

"No, we'd have to pick it up," she said. "Nah, let's look in the freezer downstairs. There might be a frozen pizza in there."

We did and there was, thankfully. Now we sat at the kitchen table waiting for the oven timer to go off.

"This feels very teenage slumber party," I remarked, smiling at her.

"I know, right? Sometimes it's fun just to hang out with nothing in particular planned. After such a busy week at school, I wasn't in the mood to go out."

"True, I understand. So, your parents went to visit your younger brother in college and then were going to Yellowstone?"

"Yeah. Three weeks on my own. I'll help with the farm work as much as I can, but we have a few guys that will do the milking, feed the animals, and whatever field work that needs to be done. I have my school schedule first, of course," she said.

"Nice," I replied. "When do you think you'll get your own place?"

"I don't know," she said as the oven timer went off. "I have it pretty good here. I don't pay rent, and Mom still does my laundry. I know, I sound like a spoiled baby. It would be nice to have my own place though. Eventually."

"Maybe when we find that sexy cop for you," I teased while she took the pizza pan out of the oven and placed it on the stove to cool.

"Yeah, when am I going to meet that guy?" She laughed. She pulled out a pizza cutter and sliced the pizza.

"We need to be on high alert," I replied. "Any old boyfriends that you can't forget?"

"Well." Robin paused. "There was someone serious in college, but it didn't work out. He got back together with his high school girlfriend. They're married now. He was the one who got away."

"The one that got away," I repeated.

"Do you have one that got away?"

I laughed. "Maybe, but it's probably best that he did."

Robin retrieved two plates from the cupboard and placed a slice of pizza on each one. "I took your advice. I told John I wasn't interested in dating him."

"Really?" I raised my eyebrows. "What happened?"

"He didn't say much. It was a few days ago, but..." she sighed. "I think I saw him parked in the school parking lot, in the back, when I left yesterday."

"Oh, no, do you think he's doing the same thing he did to your friend, Margie?"

"I hope not, and I might be wrong, but it looked like his truck. I just got out of there fast," she said, taking a bite of pizza.

I nodded, chewed my pizza and swallowed. I hoped I hadn't given Robin some bad advice. "Probably wasn't him. Let's get back to the hot cop. Maybe we should go online. Tinder?"

"Uh, nah, but we could go out to a club next week," she said. "There's a good one two towns over. Even if nobody interesting is there, it would still be fun to go out."

"We're not going to be line dancing, are we?" I asked.

She raised her eyebrows. "It's a possibility."

We laughed and worked on our pizza.

"Hey, do you have ranch dressing?" I asked. "I like to dip my pizza in it sometimes. Feeling that craving now."

"I think so. Look in the fridge," she said.

I walked over to the stainless-steel refrigerator and opened the door. I spied the ranch in the door and reached out to grab it, but something else caught my eye.

A bag of organic medjool dates. A specific brand.

I picked up the bag and turned to Robin. "Where did you get these?"

She stared at the bag. "Dates? I don't know. My parents must have gotten them. I don't like dates."

I placed the full bag back into the refrigerator, a coldness creeping up my spine.

He had been here.

A couple days passed, but by Tuesday I still couldn't get that bag of dates from Robin's refrigerator out of my mind. The exact brand, organic brand, local to California, I'd never seen that brand since moving back to Pennsylvania. And I'd looked several times. Did Robin's parents order them online? Maybe, but that seemed too coincidental.

So, that meant someone placed the dates there, knowing I would find them. How had this person known I'd be over at Robin's house last weekend? Was our house bugged, was someone listening to Archie and me? What did it mean? These stupid little gifts were just trying to weaken my sanity. Not threatening but placed to toy with my emotions and make me feel uncomfortable. Mission accomplished. Dream must be the one leaving me gifts. Brother Jim would not be toying with me this much; he didn't have the patience.

I fed the chickens, dumping their feed into their bowl, and filled the automatic water dispenser. They clucked an approval and greedily gobbled up the feed. I walked back into the barn, put the bucket away, and grabbed my watering can.

I walked onto the front porch to water the bright yellow and orange mums I planted a few days before to welcome in the fall season. A quick stroll to the back patio to water the flowers back there and I was done. I left the watering can on the patio. I planned to water the plants again in the evening; they'd been gobbling up the water, and I wanted them to stay bright and lush. I went into the house, grabbed my purse, locked the doors and headed out to the garage. I glanced at my phone. Eight forty-five. In fifteen minutes, I'd be opening the store. Rachel would be in at ten.

I got into my car, and backed out of the garage, then stopped to hit the button to close the door. A text beeped on my phone. I glanced at it. Archie.

> Hey, can you stop at Robin's house?

Weird. Why did he want me to do that? I typed a reply.

> I'm on my way to the store. Isn't she at school?

> No, and she's not answering her phone. The principal is in her class now. Neither of us have had any luck reaching her.

> Okay, I'll go over.

I backed my car around and headed out the lane to Robin's house. A few minutes later I was driving down her lane, lined with maple trees. The lights in the barn were on and the side door was open. I saw a man adjusting something on the milking machine. Two pickup trucks were parked to the side of the driveway. Probably the farm workers Robin mentioned last Saturday. Robin's car was there, in the front of the driveway. A long sidewalk led to the red brick farmhouse.

I parked and hurried up the sidewalk to the front door. I rang the doorbell, then knocked. Nothing. I called her cell. Nothing. The curtains were pulled shut so I couldn't see anything inside. What was going on? Could Robin be hurt?

I walked around to the back door that entered the kitchen. I could hear Daisy, Robin's Labrador Retriever, whimpering. I peeked into the window and saw Daisy hovering around something on the floor. My heart hammered inside my chest as I turned the doorknob and it opened. Daisy barked and bounded over to me.

Robin was lying behind the kitchen table in the center of the room. Her eyes wide and frozen with fright. Her face swollen.

She wasn't moving.

Or breathing.

THIRTY-ONE
2016

The Commune
Dream

I pulled up to Grandmother's house and parked the van in the driveway. We had a busy day at the farmers' market today, selling out of basically everything we brought. I yawned, sitting in the van for a moment. I dropped off Sunny, River, and Aurora, one of our newest members, at Raindrop's house. Sunny just wanted to lie by the pool and rest after the busy day. I was picking up Brother Jim. He planned to stay at Raindrop's house that week. I was sure Jasmine, his assistant, would also join.

I got out of the van and walked through the curved archway to the heavy, dark wooden door and entered the home. I hadn't been here for a month or two. We usually had our chanting sessions as a group at Raindrop's house because of the ample space, or in the mountains. The living room had several new pieces of furniture, large sectional, massive recliner, a huge flatscreen TV hung on the wall. I peeked into the kitchen at the back of the house: A new, large stainless-steel refrigerator was there, along with a newly installed dishwasher. Jim Bob was busy making some upgrades in the house.

A young woman walked into the living room. She was dressed in a very thin, very short, light pink cotton dress, her feet bare. She looked incredibly young. My guess barely sixteen. She smiled shyly at me with big brown eyes. She brushed back her dark blond hair.

"Hi," she said.

"Hi," I replied. "I'm Dream. I don't think we've met. What's your name?"

She giggled. Yes, my guess was right, she was young. "I'm Willow now. That's my new name. I just moved in last week."

"Nice to meet you, Willow. I usually stay at Listening Lark's other house, but this used to be my home for many years. Is Brother Jim home?"

"Yes," she said, smiling at me. "He's in his office."

Oh, this girl is way too young. I warned Jim Bob about this when we started the commune. No underage girls. "Thank you, Willow," I said.

I walked to the back of the house to Jim Bob's office. He sat in a large, dark gray wingback chair, one of Grandmother's, behind a midsize mahogany desk, also Grandmother's, and typed on his laptop.

"Hey," I said, walking inside the room. I sat on the wide jacquard patterned couch, Grandmother's favorite couch, opposite the desk.

He looked up and closed the laptop. "Dream, close the door. I want to talk a bit before we leave."

"So do I," I said. I closed the door and sat back on the couch. "I met Willow."

Jim Bob's face broke out in a wide smile. "Oh, yes, sweet Willow. She just joined us last week. She was a runaway I met at the swap meet."

"How old is she, fifteen, sixteen?"

"Eighteen."

I snorted. "She is not and you know it. You can't have underage girls here."

"I don't *know it*. She's eighteen and she's staying. Sunny isn't much older than her. She's twenty-one now, right? But she was nineteen when she joined us."

"Barely. She turned twenty a month later."

"Dream, I know what you're saying. But there are no underage girls at Listening Lark. Why are you so hung up on this? I thought you didn't want to be involved with the details. You just want to do what you do and get your money every month."

"True," I said. He was right. I didn't want to know many details, and the money I received increased every month, so Jim Bob must have known what he was doing. If Listening Lark folded, I had plenty to buy Sunny and I a nice little place, or maybe an RV to travel the country, and live out the rest of our lives; but housing underage girls would bring the cops here. We couldn't have that, especially me, and he knew all of this. That was why he handled all the details and paid me my part in cash every month. I was a ghost in the real world, but I was still an equal partner in Listening Lark with Jim Bob. I held Jim Bob's secrets, and he held mine. Loyalty existed between us not only because of our family bond, but the private matters we knew about one another. I couldn't say I liked Jim Bob in any substantial way, but I admired some of his traits, and I trusted him when it counted, at least in reference to me. Others he would screw over. I'd seen it happen many times in the past.

"Anyway, that's settled." Brother Jim sighed. "I think I must change up my group talks, sprinkle in a little more Eastern philosophy. Talk about my travels in Tibet."

"Tibet?" I laughed. "I think you mean your travels around Encino."

Jim Bob chuckled. "You know too much about me."

"We know too much about each other," I replied. "Well, the other day on the mountain was impressive. That was some costume Moonbeam made for you."

He nodded. "Good, yeah everything felt fresh and intense that day. That is the feeling I want to nurture with the family."

"I like that idea. The vibe of the group chanting on the top of the mountain was so intense."

"Yes, I agree." He cocked his head to the side. "I really want to stress the importance of us being one. Everyone sharing with one another, their earthly possessions, their gifts, their bodies. If we achieve this, it will solidify our power with them, and be very profitable, too."

"I agree to a certain point. Everything still needs to be an individual's choice; you can't bully a family member into complying with your vision. They must want it too," I said. "I know we want to make money, but it must be a choice. You can't force people."

He laughed. "Always wearing your heart on your sleeve, Dream. Of course it would be the individual's choice, but it's my job to create a desire for them to make that choice. The right choice."

Now I laughed. "You're always the persuader. Have been since we've been kids."

"And it's worked well for me. Worked well for both of us."

I nodded. "You're right."

"One other thing I've been wondering about. Raindrop and River, are they fucking each other?" Jim Bob leaned back in his chair. His eyes narrowed.

"They're really friendly, but I haven't seen them doing anything," I said. No way in hell I was telling him what Sunny said. That would only stir a hornets' nest and make things uncomfortable for everyone involved. I wasn't going to stir up that mess. I was sure he would eventually find out, but it wasn't coming from me. I could tell Jim Bob believed me, and he relaxed a bit. We discussed a few more Listening Lark issues, but I knew he wasn't going to let go of his theory about Raindrop and River.

A theory I already knew as true.

THIRTY-TWO

2023

Aimee

The police and paramedics swarmed Robin's house. Red lights blinking everywhere I looked, people standing around, talking about the victim, and staring at me. I was standing in the driveway, by my car, going over my statement with Officer Henning, when Archie drove down the lane and parked beside me. He jumped out of the car and ran over to me.

"Is she...?" He stared at me.

"Dead." I nodded, tears running from my eyes. He hugged me.

"Okay, Mrs. Greencastle," Officer Henning said. "I have everything I need. If you think of anything else, please call me. You two can head home. We'll be in touch if we need anything else." He handed me his card and walked toward the house.

"How?" Archie asked. "What happened?"

"They think she had a severe allergic reaction to something," I replied; images of her swollen face popped into my mind. I wiped the tears away from my eyes. I looked back at the house, so full of activity now. "It was awful. She was just lying on the kitchen floor. Her face was so swollen."

"But why didn't she use her EpiPen? She has them everywhere. I know she keeps one in her purse."

"I don't know. Maybe she couldn't reach them, if it happened quickly."

"This is unbelievable." He paced. "I just talked to her at school yesterday."

"I know," I agreed, staring at the house. "And I stopped over at her house yesterday."

I looked at Archie. "Do you have to go back to school?"

"No, they got a substitute to fill in for the rest of the day."

"Okay." I got into my car. "I'll see you at home."

We snuggled on the sofa together watching random TV, trying to understand how our friend, Robin, could be dead. None of this made any sense. Only this weekend we had our little slumber party, watching movies, making pizza, and now... she was gone.

We would never see her again.

I thought about her parents getting the call on their vacation in Yellowstone that their daughter was dead. Nobody should have to receive a call like that in their life. I could only imagine the shock they must have felt when they answered the phone call. They left home not even a week ago, with Robin perfectly fine and probably excited to see their son and go on vacation. Now, they had to come home and plan their daughter's funeral.

She was so careful about her nut allergy. How had she gotten something with nuts? Why hadn't she used one of her EpiPens? Like Archie mentioned, she always had one close by. None of this made any sense.

Archie's phone rang. He answered. "Hey, John, did you hear?"

I stared at him. So strange sitting here listening to Archie talk to John about Robin. The whole situation felt surreal. I hadn't known Robin very long, but I really liked her and enjoyed spending time with her. She was my only real friend here. How could she be gone?

"Oh, really," Archie said. "Okay, yeah, bye."

Archie hung up the phone. "John has a friend at the police department. Looks like it was anaphylaxis. She just stopped breathing and her heart stopped. They are testing a soup container. I guess there was an almost empty soup container in the refrigerator and a bowl, still containing some soup, lying on the floor near Robin. There was an EpiPen in the kitchen drawer and in her purse on the counter. It's crazy that she couldn't have reached one of those in time."

"Yes, it is. I can't believe we lost our friend today," I said.

Archie nodded and we stared at the TV, both lost in our own thoughts.

THIRTY-THREE
2023

Aimee

The next week, we sat in the funeral home on soft cushioned red seats watching the video montage of Robin's short life displayed on the screen. She had been a beautiful child, with long dark hair, usually up in a ponytail, and big brown eyes. There were so many photos of her on the farm, with the alpacas, grooming them, helping to feed them, showing them at a 4-H fair and winning ribbons. Photos of family Christmases and picnics.

Then the photos moved on to college, showing a bright-eyed girl studying to be a teacher. Photos of her with many friends. Graduation. Then a proud Robin stood in front of Poplin Elementary wearing her lanyard with the school ID card around her neck. Officially a teacher.

The room, filled with people, hung with sadness of the loss, many people crying and mourning a kind, beautiful young woman. This was the second funeral in Poplin in only a few months, although this one appeared accidental. Nevertheless, still a shock.

Her parents stood at the front of the room, stoic and stiff, as they hovered by their daughter's dark blue casket. Her brother, Mark, stood there too, his hands shoved into his suit pockets. A memorial candle was lit behind him on a shelf, with an image of Robin, the same as they used for the obituary. Flowers filled the space around the casket. My mind traveled back to my father's funeral. While he wasn't a great man, or even a good one, he did teach me lessons I'd used throughout my life. I sighed, wanting to push the memories back into the dark recesses of my mind.

The pastor was about to begin, and the family sat down on chairs in the front row, the room hushed. He spoke about Robin and how although her life was short, it was well lived, and how she had found peace in heaven; she would never feel the pain and suffering of this world again. And one day we would see her again.

I didn't know how to feel about his sermon. Were we supposed to be glad Robin died? No, his well-crafted message was designed to give comfort to those left behind, all of us who mourned Robin's passing. What else was he supposed to say?

Death was a part of life. Everyone knows this is true, as natural as being born, or falling in love, the circle of life. And like so many things in life, we never know when the unthinkable arrives at our door. How we deal with it is the important part: Does it make us stronger, or push us over the edge?

Archie squeezed my hand. I squeezed back, staring at him. He looked so handsome in his dark suit, black shirt, and gray striped tie. His warm brown eyes, sad but filled with love for me, made me realize how happy I was to be alive and to have him in my life. I had climbed out of my darkness a few months before meeting Archie, but the day I met him I felt an old spark light up in me, stronger than I'd been in years.

The rest of the sermon passed slowly, and I kept thinking of the time I spent with Robin. A brief friendship, but still many good times I shared with her that I would remember. Today we put her to rest, but I would miss my friend for much longer.

Robin's death was ruled accidental: Traces of peanut were found in her system, along with the last meal she ate, vegetable soup, and traces of peanut were found in the grocery store container, and also in the bowl found on the floor next to Robin that still contained remnants of the soup. The theory was that her allergic reaction was so severe it prevented her from reaching the EpiPen, two in fact, only a few feet away.

As sad as the news was, it was a bit of a relief knowing it was an accident and not a murder. Angela's death, still unsolved, hung over the town like a cloud. Two murders within a few months would induce widespread panic in the small, rural town. It would expose the truth that any place can be dangerous. There is no location that can truly be called idyllic, because danger is not in locations.

It's inside people, lurking and unpredictable when it may explode.

Sure, most people have coping skills, abilities to make rational decisions and see what the consequence of their behavior may be in the end. Some don't have those skills, and some are pushed so far over the edge that coping skills are not even a factor in their thought process.

The one thing I remembered from my brief college experience was my intro to psych class. A brief overview, but nonetheless, fascinating to open the door on all the various theories of the human psyche. Are we in control of our lives? Why do we possess certain thought patterns? And the old debate of nature versus nurture, can it be simply one that determines our destiny or rather a combination of both? Is a person born good or bad? What tips the scales in either direction?

I placed the couple of dishes sitting in the sink into the dish-

washer and closed the door. Archie was at school, but today was
Monday, so the store was closed. I retrieved a glass of water. I
had drunk too much coffee this morning already, and walked
out the back door to the covered patio. I got comfortable in the
soft, floral, Hawaiian-style cushioned chair close to the fire pit
and stared at the open fields now surrounding me. John cut the
corn last weekend and now all that was left were nubs and a few
stray stalks. Our view, now seemingly endless under vast blue
skies and rolling blue mountains in the distance. A gentle
breeze kissed my skin, and the call of birds provided a pleasant
melody.

The apple trees by the garden, pregnant with fruit, caught
my eye. I would have to pick those today to take into the store
tomorrow. Maybe I would make homemade applesauce today or
apple crisp. There were a few pear trees, too. In the spring, I
wanted to plant more fruit trees.

I drank my water and pondered about all the recent events.
Life was so unpredictable. Maybe Listening Lark had it right,
live in the here and now. You never know when your time is up.
Think of all the time you waste on preparing for the future,
especially if your future is taken away from you, and it can be at
any time.

After I left Listening Lark and moved back in with Aunt
Lou I fell into a deep depression. For almost three years, I struggled, sometimes barely getting out of bed for days or taking a
shower. I remembered once going weeks without a shower.
Finally, I couldn't stand my stink. Showering and washing my
hair felt like a spa treatment that day. Unbelievably good, but I
went through the entire cycle again. And again. Aunt Lou tried
to help, but she had her own health and mental struggles. She
was almost eighty years old, my mother's older sister.

It happened slowly. My return to the world. I started
sleeping less, showering more, and focusing on things that made
me feel something. A good book. A good meal. A funny movie. I

made sure to practice self-care, exercising, particularly yoga, moisturizing my skin, putting on a bit of makeup, styling my hair. Those small actions made me feel alive. I also began seeing a psychiatrist and the medication she prescribed proved helpful for me. I started going to local farmers' markets, perusing the fresh produce and other treats. Their vibrant colors and scents made me happy, and I began cooking meals at home, much to Aunt Lou's delight, and baking tasty treats.

I got a job at a local coffee shop just to be around people my age, and I liked it. I worked with nice people, although none I would call a friend, but pleasant acquaintances to enjoy a conversation with here and there. At that point that was all I needed. Nothing too close.

Shortly after I started my job, Archie walked into the coffee shop and my life changed again. Funny how the people you end up having a strong connection with are the people you don't expect. They walk into your life, and you realize you've been waiting for them to show up. Oh, hello. I've been looking and hoping for you for such a long time.

Archie was taking Robin's death hard. Probably harder than me, which I guess made sense since he worked with her every day. I'm sure it was very strange to go to school every day and have someone else teaching in her classroom. I remembered going into school and helping her set up the bulletin boards. When I thought of it now, it seemed like years ago, not just a couple months.

On the plus side, I hadn't received any strange gifts or experienced anything unusual in our house over the last few weeks. As thankful as I was for the silence, I entertained the thought that it might only be the calm before the storm. I still thought about that bag of dates in Robin's refrigerator. Too familiar. Too coincidental for that exact brand to be in there. Did their presence have something to do with Robin's death? Was it a warning to me, or a prelude to the act? Even though Robin's death was ruled accidental, a lingering worry inside me thought this may not be the truth. There were no facts I could point to, but only a feeling I could not shake and grew stronger within me every day. For the first time, I was feeling truly scared about what this person wanted. I wondered if I should tell Archie about my past and the odd things that had been happening lately, but I knew that I wouldn't.

Some secrets shouldn't be shared.

Even with your husband. Even if you love him very much.

THIRTY-FOUR

2023

Aimee

The cool, chilly days of autumn gave the promise of crackling fires, warm holidays, cozy clothing, and the hope of a magical snowfall. Okay, I guess most people didn't consider a snowfall magical, but I did. When I was a kid, I loved waking up to snow falling outside my window and if it was a school day, hoped and prayed that we would receive a phone call that school was closed for the day, leaving me free to build snowmen and snow forts. As an adult, I loved having a hot cup of something, coffee, tea, hot chocolate, whatever, and watching the snow fall outside my window, covering everything with its magic fairy dust. Snow was the one thing I missed in California.

It was mid-November now, two months since Robin's death. Business at the store was booming with the fall harvest, pumpkins, gourds, and apples selling out most days. My baked goods were now pumpkin bread, apple and pumpkin muffins, and pumpkin cake with cream cheese icing. Archie made a few more items too, two benches—one sold, one left—and some cute wooden jack-o'-lanterns that sold out the first day I brought them in.

Today I stocked butternut squash, cauliflower and winter squash, the butternut squash quite an abundant crop. The pumpkins lining the front wall were almost all gone now. All the large ones were bought in the Halloween rush for carving pumpkins. Only the smaller ones and some of the tiny Jack B Littles, my personal favorites, were left.

"Aimee, would you like me to put the jams on the shelf?" Rachel asked. She adjusted her black bonnet.

I looked over to her, standing by the cash register. "Yes, that would be great. Thanks, Rachel."

Hiring Rachel had been a good move on my part. She was a hard worker, always on time and very reliable. If I had something going on and couldn't make it into the store, she was always willing to step in and cover the store for me. She was also a very nice person.

I missed Robin. I missed having a girlfriend to gossip with and talk about silly things. The closest I had to a girlfriend now was Rachel, but our conversations didn't go much beyond food and the weather. I didn't see her going out for drinks or talking about hot cops. She invited me to go to an ice cream social at her church last month. Thoughtful of her to ask, but not really my scene.

The bell jingled. I looked over and smiled.

My smile froze on my face.

John.

I turned to him. "Hello," I greeted in what I hoped was a friendly tone.

"Hi, Aimee," he said, smiling widely. He turned to Rachel, still stocking the apple jam. "Hi, Rachel."

"Hello," she said demurely.

John walked over to Rachel. "What kind of jam is that?"

She held up a jar. "Apple."

"I'll take two of those, please," he said, taking two from the shelf.

Rachel nodded and went back to stocking.

I stared at him as he walked around the store, picking up a bunch of cauliflower, eggs, a container of goat's milk hand lotion, and a box of homemade chocolate candies.

John had been acting truly weird lately. It seemed as if he had transferred his creepy lurking previously saved for Robin over to me, and possibly Rachel, although it may just have been that she was usually around. He stopped in frequently at the store, often hanging around when we closed and walking out with us. Lingering long after he purchased his items. Moving uncomfortably close to me when having a conversation. I had mentioned it to Archie, but of course he hadn't noticed anything.

I went to the register and rang up his purchases.

"How's business?" he asked.

I smiled. He should know. He was in here every other day. How much jam could he and his grandma eat?

"Busy."

"I'm surprised Archie's other bench hasn't sold yet," he remarked. "Grandma and I love ours."

"Glad to hear it," I replied. I handed him the bag. "I'm sure it will sell by Christmas."

"Hard to believe Thanksgiving is just around the corner," he said, picking up the bag.

"Sure is. Have a good day, John," I said, trying to nudge him out the door.

"What are you and Archie doing for Thanksgiving?"

"Making turkey like everyone else," I replied. When was this guy going to leave?

"Are you having company over?"

"Um... maybe. Not sure yet."

"Okay, what about you, Rachel?"

"Having dinner with my family," she replied in a quiet voice.

The door jingled and two customers walked in. Saved by the bell. Thank goodness.

"Thanks, John, have a good day," I repeated, hurrying over to the customers.

John finally got the hint and left the store. After the other customers exited, with bags of squash and homemade yogurt, Rachel wiped the counter by the cash register.

"Are you friends with that John guy?" she asked.

"My husband is," I said vaguely.

She nodded. "He's strange, I think. My mom says stay away from him; he's an odd one."

"I think your mom is right," I agreed. "He is an odd one." Well, it was good to know I wasn't the only one who found John unsettling. Rachel's mother sensed it too and warned her daughter. I still didn't understand why Archie couldn't see it.

My cell phone rang shrilly and I glanced at it. Poplin National Bank. I wondered what they wanted. "Hello?"

"Hello, this is Alice calling from Poplin National Bank. Is this Aimee Greencastle?"

"Yes."

"Mrs. Greencastle, there is an overdraft on your checking account this morning in the amount of two thousand, seven hundred twenty-three dollars and forty-five cents. Will you be able to cover that today?"

"Overdraft, what? How has that happened?"

"Give me a moment," Alice said. A minute or two passed.

"Okay, your husband transferred fifty thousand dollars from the business account to the personal. That is what caused the overdraft."

"Oh, um, I thought we had overdraft protection with our savings account."

"No, I don't see that you signed up for that. Do you think you could stop in and sign that agreement authorizing us to pull funds from your savings? You could do it online too if you choose."

"I'll come in. I'll be there soon. Thank you, Alice." I clicked off my phone.

I called Archie.

"Hello?"

"What's up with the fifty-thousand-dollar transfer from the business account? It overdrew the account. The bank just called."

"Oh, shit, sorry. I thought we had more in that account. I had to pay for that side-by-side ATV we ordered. Remember we talked about it?"

"It cost fifty thousand dollars?"

"No, but close to thirty. Then we had other expenses coming up like insurance bills and those repairs for the barn, that kind of stuff. I just thought it would be easier to transfer enough for everything."

"Oh, okay, when do we get the ATV?"

"This weekend. It'll be so much fun to drive around. We can even drive it into town." Archie's voice was tinged with excitement; it was nice to hear him so jolly.

"Okay, well I have to go to the bank to sign a paper," I said.

"Sorry, babe. Look I've got to go, but I promise it'll be worth it." Archie hung up.

I stared at the phone, walked out to my car, and headed to the bank.

THIRTY-FIVE

2023

Aimee

Blanketing the world outside my window was the first frost of the year. Icy little pockets covered the dead grass and the fields beyond creating a magical looking fairyland. A fire crackled from our living room fireplace, the mantle decorated with bright orange pumpkins, yellow gourds, and creamy white candles, softly flickering.

Archie and I nursed our coffees and ate buttered toast with apple jam. Nothing too heavy since we'd be eating a large meal later. I'd planned to make Thanksgiving dinner here, just the two of us, but John had invited us to dinner with him and his grandma, and Archie accepted, much to my annoyance, without checking with me first. I decided to brush it off and enjoy the day, even if spending time with John wasn't something I relished. I hadn't met his grandma yet, so hopefully she was pleasant. I told Archie I was spending two hours there, tops, and then we're out of there. And this would be the only holiday I'd be spending with John. I could only imagine him wanting us to get matching Christmas jammies and opening presents together on Christmas morning.

Oh, hell no.

I had some serious concerns about Archie's lack of insight toward John. He thought he was such a great guy. A good friend. But if Rachel and her mother could recognize that John was odd and to keep your distance, how was he oblivious to it? Is it only women who hold a particular instinct about certain men?

Archie got up and put another log on the fire. He settled down next to me on the sofa. "This is nice."

"Mmmm... it is," I agreed, sipping my coffee.

I took another bite of toast while Archie flicked through TV channels and settled on the Macy's Thanksgiving Day Parade. I watched the floats travel down the street, but my mind wandered to the last two months.

So quiet.

So very quiet.

No strange gifts, or photos had arrived. Nothing unusual at the house. Life was normal, and that was weird, given the circumstances. Why would someone go to the trouble of doing those things, with the intention to scare me, I'm sure, just to disappear. All of it appeared so pointless.

And also... why disappear after Robin's death?

I had entertained the idea, briefly, that Robin had something to do with the things that were happening to me, even though my gut told me it was Dream, but that theory held no logic. She had no ties to Listening Lark, I was certain. She would have been sixteen or seventeen and showing animals at the 4-H fair when I lived in the commune with Dream. There was no way she was leaving the strange items for me to discover. There was another possibility about the unknown individual.

That maybe they were in mourning.

For Robin.

John?

I didn't know of any connection he'd have to Listening Lark either, but what did I really know about him? Was it possible he knew Dream? He was older than me, maybe early thirties.

Robin had said he'd lived in Poplin with his grandma for a long time. But where were his parents? How long is a long time? That time span could be a lifetime, or five years. I'd be digging in at dinner today. Hopefully his grandma would like to talk.

John and his grandma lived in a small ranch house, just outside of town, the opposite way from our farm. It was a tidy tan siding house with dark cranberry shutters and a matching cranberry front door. Bright yellow mums, a bit deflated from the morning's frost, sat in a large tan plastic planter. A homemade grapevine wreath hung on the front door.

John answered the door, a wide smile on his face. "Happy Thanksgiving, Greencastles!"

"Happy Thanksgiving!" Archie and I said in unison.

We walked into the neat as a pin house. The front door opened to a comfortable living room with two beige floral sofas and a large, overstuffed chair, and an oval, well-loved coffee table in the center. A large flatscreen TV hung on the far wall.

An older woman, not as old as I expected, walked out of the kitchen. She was a petite woman with short salt-and-pepper hair, wearing khaki pants and a pretty, sparkly deep brown sweater. She smiled at us in a friendly way.

"Oh, hello," she greeted warmly. "I'm Debra—Welcome! Happy Thanksgiving."

"Thank you for inviting us," I said. I handed her a bouquet of fall flowers, and Archie gave John a pumpkin roll.

"Thank you," Debra said. "Oh, pumpkin roll is one of my favorites. Did you make it, Aimee?"

"Yes, I did, it's one of Archie's favorites too." I laughed.

John hung up our coats, and we proceeded to the combination kitchen and dining room. Older, dark cabinets lined the walls, beige laminate kitchen counters, plain light beige linoleum stretched out on the floor, somewhat worn, but gleaming clean.

A large country blue braided rug sat atop the linoleum. A rectangular dining table, with six padded chairs, sat on the rug. The table had a bright orange and yellow plaid tablecloth and was set with cream colored dinnerware. A tall hutch, painted the same color as the rug, stood against the wall filled with various dishes and bric-a-brac. Delicious smells filled the room.

Debra placed the flowers into a vase and put them in the center of the well-laid table. "They look beautiful."

"Some wine?" John offered.

Archie and I accepted the glasses, nodding our appreciation.

"I'm so glad you two could join us." Debra smiled. "You're such good friends with my Johnny."

"Johnny?" I asked, raising my eyebrows.

John laughed. "Grandma's the only one who calls me Johnny."

"Maybe I'll start," Archie teased.

"Nope," John retorted.

I turned to Debra. "Our pleasure. So nice to finally meet you. John talks about you often."

Debra smiled. "I keep meaning to stop in at your store, but Johnny stops in after work to get what I need. One of these days."

"Yeah, that would be great," I replied. I'd much rather see Debra than "Johnny."

"Shall we eat?" Debra motioned to the table. "Everything is ready."

. . .

Dinner proved to be a wonderful feast and Debra an upbeat and interesting conversationalist. She was a retired emergency room nurse, a single mother to John's mother and a son who died as a teenager in a car accident. She volunteered at the local humane society and liked to take painting classes. I really liked her. She was nothing like John. John, on the other hand, was polite and seemingly friendly when we were in a group, but when we passed each other in the hallway as I walked to the bathroom, he glared at me in a most unfriendly way. Obviously, he was putting on a show for his grandma and Archie. His behavior toward me was downright disturbing.

The dinner dishes were cleared away, and we were drinking coffee with pumpkin pie and pumpkin roll, our bellies bursting as they did every Thanksgiving Day.

"Oh, Johnny, I remember how your mom loved pumpkin pie," Debra said. "I always had to make sure to make two pies, so everyone got some."

"I know, Grandma." John nodded.

I sipped my coffee. "Where is your mom, John?"

A silence fell over the room for a moment, and I quickly regretted asking the question.

"Well, my daughter left when Johnny was two years old. She was a young single mother, like me, but she wanted a different life." Debra paused. "She knew I would take care of her Johnny."

"Where did she go?" Archie asked.

I wasn't the only one who asked awkward questions.

"I don't know, she just left," said Debra. "She told me to take care of Johnny and she'd be in touch. We've never heard a peep from her. Nothing, not even a Christmas card or a birthday gift for Johnny. I pray that she's doing well."

Archie and I nodded, finishing our dessert. John got up to retrieve more wine.

Christmas at the Commune
Dream

Magic was in the air at Listening Lark, Christmas magic. I sat at the small kitchen table in the guesthouse eating scrambled eggs and drinking pineapple juice. We put a chicken coop on Raindrop's land, past the yoga deck, in the small grove of trees, to give the chickens shade from the hot SoCal sun. They were great producers, and Sunny and I had fresh eggs for breakfast every morning.

A tall, curved, metal palm tree with wide green fabric leaves brightened by white lights on the trunk and leaves sat by the small gas fireplace. Multicolored lights hung around the ficus tree on the other side. Stockings, one for Sunny and one for me, decked the fireplace. A stuffed snowman and snowwoman, holding hands, sat under the tree. Raindrop's attic was filled with Christmas decorations. When River and I went up to retrieve ornaments and lights for the nine-foot Douglas fir we placed in the main living room, we brought down several more items, maybe going a little crazy with the decorations and lights, but everyone in the family enjoyed the festive look. Sunny loved the palm tree and snow people, so we enjoyed those in our guesthouse.

Sunny still slept in our bed, her long blonde hair barely visible under the white down comforter and pillows. Last night was a late one, probably around two when we fell asleep. She would sleep well past the normal time she got up, which was fine; we made our own schedule here. I, for one, could never stick to a rigid schedule like most people seem to do. I liked to live a fluid life.

Christmas was next week. Brother Jim planned a big celebration for the entire family on Christmas Eve at Raindrop's house. It would be interesting to have everyone here overnight. We would set up tents outside for those who did not want to stay indoors; some members preferred the outdoors. I was one of those people until we moved to the guesthouse. I think it was more a matter of having privacy with Sunny than an indoor or outdoor preference. I loved living there, and hoped our existence in the guesthouse lasted a very long time.

Jim Bob was getting more suspicious about River. Lately, he'd been keeping him at Grandmother's house more frequently, working on projects around the house with Eagle. He wanted to keep a strong hold on Raindrop; she was our biggest financial supporter, and had just begun filming a movie that was supposed to be a huge blockbuster. That meant more money for Listening Lark and more areas for Brother Jim to expand into and grow our family. Jim Bob called me yesterday. Two new members to the family would join us for the Christmas Eve celebration. Both who would secure more substantial financial support, a model, one of Raindrop's friends, and an executive in the fashion industry. He was doing exactly what he told me he would do. Listening Lark was growing by the day.

.   .   .

On Christmas Eve, the house twinkled with lights and the backyard twinkled more. Alternating strings of white and multi-colored lights hung around the pool, outdoor dining space, and farther back on the Zen Yoga Deck. The guesthouse was draped in lights, looking like a fairytale house outside the main house that burst with Christmas cheer—from the tall tree in the main living room decorated in silver and blue to the smaller trees in the dining room and family room. Raindrop was a bit of a Christmas fanatic, and with our help, created a house perfect for any Christmas elf.

Sunny and I were busy baking today, making batches of cookies not with sugar, but agave and other natural sweeteners. I loved watching her as we baked, the delicate gold heart locket I bought her for Christmas hung on her slim neck. I couldn't wait to give it to her, so we exchanged gifts early. She loved the locket and I the leather-bound journal she bought for me. The universe sent me the perfect woman. She knew how much I loved to write in my journal every day.

Brother Jim had a huge white tent set up past the yoga deck, decorated in white lights and a large Christmas tree, adorned with white lights, and flocked with fake snow. I was surprised he was putting in so much effort for the holiday, although most of it was fueled by Raindrop. Our Christmases in the past had been festive, but low key compared to this year. Brother Jim had a big announcement tonight. I thought I knew what it was, but sometimes he surprised even me, and we were supposed to be partners. I was sure he'd have liked to be the sole owner of Listening Lark, but that wasn't the case. We kept each other in check, well, most of the time.

We gathered under the tent's twinkling white lights among all the family members, almost seventy now. We wore our white robes with gold embroidery, and Brother Jim stepped up on the small, elevated platform, white lights hanging vertically behind him, giving him a white glow. He was dressed in a white gown; his long raven hair, same color as mine but sparser with his receding hairline, flowed down his back. He raised his arms high, eyes to the heavens, and began to chant. The crowd followed suit.

"Family," he said in a strong, yet soothing, hypnotic voice. "Brothers and sisters of Listening Lark. As we celebrate tonight and look forward to the future, the universe has provided opportunities for us. As we travel our path to spiritual oneness, we as the individual open to become part of a whole living organism. And I know you can feel the beating heart tonight of oneness. Look around, brothers and sisters, feel the bodies and spirits of us blend to form Listening Lark. An outpouring of sharing and harmony joining everything we have with one another. Shout it! Shout it!"

Brother Jim raised his arms higher, doing the angel wing pose again. The white lights behind him seemingly glowing even brighter than when he started talking, making him seem even more angelic. Damn, he was a good performer.

"Listening Lark! Listening Lark!" the crowd shouted over and over again.

"Louder!" he commanded, his arms still raised.

"Listening Lark! Listening Lark!" Voices became bolder and louder as they echoed off one another.

Sunny and I joined the shouting and chanting. Being in a group like this with the raw energy vibrating through it was intoxicating to me, even if I knew it was a ruse. I didn't care. The feeling of the moment filled me with such fervor, I got lost in it.

Brother Jim put his hands up to indicate silence. "And, so, I'm happy to announce we are buying the property adjacent to Raindrop's house, so that we can truly live together as a family! This is a new day for Listening Lark!"

The crowd clapped and cheered, some dancing around. I smiled, already knowing the news. The new member, the fashion executive, had deep pockets, and wanted to lavish it on Listening Lark, much to Jim Bob's delight. Grandmother's house now would be used for office and work purposes. Jim Bob wanted to expand Moonbeam's jewelry making business, with Lilac's help, and start making homemade wine as a family business, as well.

"I'm also delighted to introduce you to three new family members," Brother Jim said. "First, welcome, Fire."

A well-groomed middle-aged man with sleek blond hair walked to the front. Must be the fashion executive.

"Star," said Brother Jim. A beautiful young redhead joined them. Must be the model.

"And, finally, Venus." Brother Jim beamed.

A young woman, slightly taller than Sunny, with long dark hair walked to the front. She turned, her tan skin glowing under the white twinkling lights, her lithe body draped in the white gown we all wore. Her wide, dark eyes stared into the crowd. Her full, red lips curved into a shy smile.

My breath stilled and I stared.

Venus.

THIRTY-SEVEN
2023

Aimee

Snow fell lightly as I left the store, my hands full of shopping bags and much-needed Christmas wrapping paper and tape. When the store from Elmville called to say the tools ordered for Archie had come in, I made a quick dash over to pick them up. After all, it was Christmas Eve. I thought I'd have to wrap up empty boxes with pictures of what I ordered: Now I'd have the actual presents to wrap.

The snow increased its intensity on the thirty-minute drive home. We planned to go to the candlelight service at the local church in Poplin, but if this kept up, we may stay home. Getting stuck along the road in a snowdrift was not on my Christmas Eve to-do list.

I pulled into our lane, stopped at the mailbox to pick up the mail, and scurried back inside the vehicle. Back in the warmth of the car, I sorted through it. A bill, two Christmas cards, junk mail. One card was from Robin's parents, a beautiful sparkling Christmas tree on the front. Sadness stabbed me as thoughts of Robin filled my mind. I was still surprised how much I missed her since we'd only known each other for a few months. But she was often in my thoughts.

The second card was from Nick, Archie's only friend. I tore open the card, a lovely snowy scene on the front. Inside, a simple, *Merry Christmas, Nick*. I flipped the envelope over and read the Oregon address. A post office box, not a street address. It occurred to me I didn't even know Nick's last name, which was a bit odd. I needed to ask Archie more about him. Maybe we should invite him to stay with us for a visit. I'd like to get to know him.

I drove up the lane, enjoying the beauty of our home. Lights were on inside the lower window; Archie was working on our Christmas Eve dinner: roast turkey, mashed potatoes, gravy, candied carrots, escarole salad, and buttery rosemary rolls. Twinkling electric candles blazed in every window. Bright snowflake lights were hung on the rails of the porch and our sparkling Christmas tree peeked out of the living room window. Snow continued to fall, blanketing the high, pitched roof, draping over the stained-glass window of the attic, spilling over the wide porch where two small pine trees, decked in bright white lights, flanked the front door. Something else sat on the front porch to the right side.

I looked closer, but the snow fell heavily now, obscuring a clear view. I parked the car in the garage, grabbed my bags and while I usually would enter through the side door, I walked onto the front porch instead.

I wiped snowflakes from my face, the wind nipping at me now as I stared at the stuffed snowman and snowwoman holding hands by our front door. Almost an exact match to the ones Dream and I had in our cozy guesthouse that one Christmas so many years ago. I placed the shopping bags down and walked over to the snow people. I examined them, so similar to the ones I remembered, but these were obviously brand new. I shivered, but it wasn't because of the cold. Tears formed in my eyes thinking of the day Dream and I decorated the guesthouse. How I had loved him. I brushed them away. It had started again. The gifts. But why after months of quiet had this new reminder of Listening Lark turned up? Dream was playing games again. I clutched my abdomen remembering the last time I saw him. How could I still have such love for him and such terror? I only wished I knew the rules of this game.

I stared at the snow people. I remembered Christmas Eve at Raindrop's house. After Raindrop gave me the key to the guest-house, we had a few brief conversations about Brother Jim and Listening Lark. Raindrop was older than most of us: She was thirty-three, but looked much younger. She was like an older sister to me, even though I was often the one giving her advice. We became close friends.

Brother Jim wasn't what he portrayed to his followers. Rain-drop found that out, and she wanted out of the relationship and out of Listening Lark. Not only to be free of Brother Jim, but to be with River. They were in love and wanted to start a life together without Listening Lark. When the property next to her went up for sale, Brother Jim demanded she buy it for the family. He had been becoming increasingly demanding of her, trying to keep his hold over her, probably sensing she knew who he really was—not the gracious leader of Listening Lark he portrayed himself to be in front of others, but an opportunist trying to grab at anything he could get a hold of, despite the damage he caused in the process, and an abuser. She tried talking to his other women, but none would listen to her, branding her as a troublemaker, and not believing in Brother Jim's mission. She refused to buy the property, and I remember my gut-wrenching sadness when she showed me all the bruises on her body. After that, we brainstormed ideas about who could help her break free of Brother Jim's hold.

I knew Dream wouldn't help. Relaxed and mellow Dream hated violence, but he'd never go against his cousin. A secrecy and bond existed between Brother Jim and Dream, one that he didn't share, even with me. In a way, I had admired the loyalty at the time because I thought it was reflective of Dream's loyalty to me. I wasn't at Listening Lark because I believed all the dogma the group presented. I was there because I wanted to be with Dream, who I loved deeply and would follow wherever he went. I liked our lifestyle and the energy of Listening Lark, but Dream was my obsession. What he wanted, I wanted. Yes, I was naïve. I didn't see what was right in front of me. I should have noticed the signs.

Then Brother Jim announced the purchase of the property next door to the family, and thunderous excitement of chanting and cheering filled the night air. I still remember the look of terror on Raindrop's face when he made the announcement. She would need to move fast to free herself from Brother Jim.

The peaceful feeling I had earlier dissipated, and I stared at the snow people again. The wind picked up and I pulled my scarf up closer to my chin. I picked the people up and examined them, nothing unusual, then searched the porch for any other clues. I surveyed the snow in the yard around the porch, but there were no footprints. Whoever left these had walked up the sidewalk, dropped them there, and left. Had Archie noticed anyone in the driveway?

Uneasiness trickled through me. I was absolutely certain this wasn't Brother Jim. He wouldn't remember the snow people. Only Dream would remember something like that, remembering what fun we had decorating that Christmas and being together. He'd remember every detail, the same as I did. I still thought of him every day, even before the strange gifts started appearing. I wished I didn't. How can someone who hurt you so badly still hold a large part of your heart? But he was inside my house, inside the store, and he knew everything about me. The one thing about a toxic relationship is that it never dies. It only lies simmering for a time and then its tentacles strengthen and grip you over and over again, without mercy.

What does he want now?

"Hey." The front door opened, and Archie poked his head outside. "I thought I heard the garage door go, but then I wondered because you never came inside. What are you doing?" He picked up the shopping bags.

"Don't look in there!" I warned him, shaking off my worries. Right now, with Archie, I was safe. "I have to wrap those!"

He laughed. "Oh, okay."

I gave one last glance to the snow people before going inside the warm house.

Christmas Eve was a perfect package wrapped in a red bow. Just me and Archie eating dinner together, listening to Christmas songs by a warm fire. We never made it to the church candlelight service, as the snow continued to fall heavily outside our windows. Six to eight inches were predicted by morning. I put the snow people out of my mind for the evening.

Archie and I exchanged presents; we didn't want to wait until tomorrow morning. Gorgeous diamond stud earrings for me and woodworking tools for him. We cuddled under our seven-foot Douglas fir teeming with white lights and various baubles of silver and gold.

Now, well past midnight, we were cozy under a fuzzy blanket, drinking hot chocolate and munching on Christmas cutout sugar cookies.

"This is everything I ever wanted," I remarked, licking a bit of whipped cream from my lip.

"It's pretty good," Archie replied, staring at the fire. "Better than I imagined."

"You weren't sure about moving here at first, were you?" I asked.

He shook his head. "Not really. I never wanted to live in the country, but now that I do, I like it. The school is great, but I wish Robin was still here." There was a wistfulness in his voice.

"So do I," I replied, searching his face.

We sat in quiet peacefulness for a bit, draining our hot chocolate, remnants now sitting in stained cups on the coffee table, and drifted off to sleep, both warm under our large fuzzy blanket.

The next morning, I woke up before Archie. I sneaked out from under the warm blanket, grabbed the tray of used mugs and cookie crumbs to deposit them into the sink. Wind howled outside. The trees blew from side to side with its force as it whipped around the branches. I peeked out the kitchen window to a fairytale world covered in icy, white snow. Snow hung on the barn, the trees, and the power lines. Hopefully the power wouldn't go out today, although we did have a generator for short-term use. I was about to turn away from the window, but I noticed footsteps in the snow going around the perimeter of the house. Not a full footprint impression, due to the strong winds swirling the snow, but footprints, none-theless.

I hurried over to the back door—more footprints, slowly being dissolved by the wind, around the corner to the door and then out the door around the other side of the house. I grasped the handle and turned. It wasn't locked. The door had been unlocked all night. *Damn it, Archie.* He was supposed to check all the doors before we went to bed.

I stomped into the living room, where he was already awake.

"Come look at this," I said. "You never locked the back door last night. There are footsteps around the house. Someone could be in here."

"Show me." He quickly jumped up. "We should have put security cameras in. I knew we should have done that." He then pulled on boots and grabbed a coat from the laundry room.

"You should have locked the stupid door!"

"Sorry, I'll check it out," he said. "Then I'll check the house. Why don't you make some coffee?"

I sighed and watched him go out the door. I got the coffee going, and he was back in a few minutes.

"Okay, looks like the footsteps go down the driveway, but no car tracks and not many footprints left either with this wind," he reported, taking off the boots and coat. "So, it looks like whoever was here did leave, but I'm going to check the house now. Every part."

And he did. From attic to basement and every nook and cranny in between and found nobody and nothing unusual. Thank goodness.

We drank coffee at the kitchen table as the wind howled outside. Little pieces of ice patted against the windows. Archie took an English muffin out of the toaster. He smeared butter on it and put half on a plate for me. I watched the butter melt into the muffin before I took a bite.

"I'm sorry I didn't lock the door," he said. "I'll feed the chickens. Why don't you take a shower?"

"Okay," I agreed. We finished our muffins and mugs of coffee, then went our separate ways.

I was irritated by the presence of the footprints and that he hadn't locked the door, even though he apologized; but the house was clear, and the doors were locked now. I guessed I needed to check to see if they were locked every night; I couldn't trust him to do it.

I went upstairs, brushed my teeth, and put the water on in the shower to warm up. I heard Archie come inside for something and then the door slammed shut downstairs as he went to feed the chickens. I walked into our bedroom and opened my underwear drawer. A white box lay atop my underwear. A red ribbon was wrapped around it.

I glanced around the room. I was alone. I opened the ribbon, allowing it to fall to the floor.

I lifted the lid of the box.

A delicate gold heart locket was inside. Almost the same as the necklace Dream got me many years ago.

The necklace I lost in the canyon.

The Commune

Dream

It had been a weird week for so many reasons. Sunny had been going off with Raindrop for private chats several times, which was unlike her. They did talk, but I wasn't sure what all the privacy was about lately. My gut told me it was nothing good. The purchase of the property next door was supposed to be finalized next week. Fire paid cash for it, so that shortened the paperwork and overall settlement time, much to Jim Bob's delight. I hadn't toured the house yet, but had walked to the edge of Raindrop's property and checked it out. It was a one-acre lot with a modern ranch-style home, smaller than Rain-drop's house, with three bedrooms and three bathrooms. A kidney-shaped pool in the backyard with a well-landscaped area around it. A big swing set to the left of the property. I wasn't sure who would use the swing set, although two family members were pregnant, so it would probably be needed at some point.

After the purchase of the property, Brother Jim sparked with ideas about buying more real estate in the area, particularly anything attaching to the current locations. His vision was a complex built on many acres of land, owned by Listening Lark to facilitate all the family members.

The complex would have a cathedral, a gym, pool, and sauna. There would be a communal eating space and a bunk house for those members without a permanent housing assignment, mostly a place for new members until sleeping arrangements were made.

His plan sounded wonderful and expensive. I was sure he had some future family members lined up with the money to finance all of his dreams. Who knew how far Brother Jim could take Listening Lark? I was happy to be along for the ride.

Venus moved into Raindrop's house. She shared a room with Harmony, Willow, and Star. She was a yoga instructor and led the morning yoga that week on the outdoor deck. She was a very good instructor and very wonderful to watch in every position. My attraction to her engulfed me.

I struggled to keep my distance from Venus, to view her only as a fellow family member. I didn't know how long I could continue because my attraction to her grew daily, and I felt myself drawn to her as if by the universe itself. I loved Sunny and promised it was only her and I forever. I needed to keep that promise, to be honorable, but I wasn't sure if I would, or could, but I knew it was so important to Sunny. The pull I felt toward Venus was electric, just as it was for Sunny. How could I ignore something so powerful? If the universe spoke to me in such a direct way, how could I not answer its call?

Sunny walked out of the house and joined me by the pool. She wore her yellow bikini.

"Where were you?" I asked.

"Talking to Raindrop," she said in a low voice.

"Again? What's going on with you two?"

Sunny looked at me, indecision covering her beautiful face.

"Tell me," I said.

She motioned for me to follow her into the guesthouse and closed the door behind her. She stared at me.

"Raindrop wants to leave Listening Lark." She paused. "And get away from Brother Jim."

"What?" I yelled in total surprise. "I hope you're trying to talk her out of it!"

She shushed me and shook her head. "No, why would I? He's terrible to her. You should see all the bruises he leaves on her. And she's in love with River."

"What the fuck, Sunny," I said, pacing the floor. "If she leaves, we leave too. She's not going to want us staying in her guesthouse."

"I know," she replied. "But we'll move back to your grand mother's house, or maybe the new house."

Anger surged through me. "I don't want to do that. I love living here."

"You should talk to your cousin. He should not be abusing women like that," she said in a sharp voice.

"I agree, but he won't listen to me."

"Maybe we should go to the police," she suggested, looking at me with questioning eyes.

"No!" I roared, a bit louder than I intended. I grabbed her arm and squeezed hard, intentionally. "No cops!"

"Dream," she snapped, pulling her arm away. "You're hurting me."

"I'm sorry." I wrapped my arms gently around her. "Please, no cops. We'll figure this out."

She hugged me back but watched me carefully. I had surprised her again, like that day in the mountains, I knew. I'd done such a good job at maintaining balance, maintaining calm, ignoring those whispers of rage still lurking within me. I was a different man now, wasn't I? Another peek of that part of me I kept hidden during our time together. I could feel myself lose control, bit by bit, that last week or so. Venus, now this, I needed to get back to my peaceful state. The past would not return.

I lived in the here and now.

THIRTY-NINE
2023

Aimee

"Thank you," I said, handing a full bag to the customer. "We'll see you in the spring." We were finishing up our big sale, fifty percent off all items in the store, during the week between Christmas and New Year's. The store would close over the winter and reopen in April. Most of the merchandise had sold, only a few straggling items remaining. Whatever was left, I'd send home with Rachel.

I looked forward to having a few months off. I wanted to try making jewelry, and if I was any good, I could sell my creations in the store. I'd start simple with bracelets and see how it went. Maybe expand to necklaces and earrings.

"The sale was a success," Rachel remarked. A spring of loose hair escaped her bonnet, and she shoved it back.

"Definitely," I said. "Almost done here and we'll close for the year. Will you come back and work for me in April?"

"Yeah, I will," she replied. "I'm going to miss coming here. It will be a boring winter and I'm on rumspringa."

"You are?" I looked at her. "I thought when Amish kids go on rumspringa they go to the big city to party and do whatever they want to do."

"Some do. Three of my friends got an apartment in Philly. One went to New York with her sister; but I don't want to go to a city. I did go shopping and bought some English clothes. It was fun wearing jeans, sneakers, and a tank top!" Rachel giggled.

"You wild woman," I teased, good-naturedly. Rachel was a sweet girl. For her, wearing a tank top was risqué and edgy. I couldn't imagine what she'd think about my time in the commune.

"Archie and I are having a New Year's Eve party," I said. "You're invited if you'd like to come. I can drive you, and you're welcome to stay overnight if you like. There will be drinking though, so if you do want to leave, you'll have to have someone pick you up."

"Oh, a real New Year's Eve party with champagne?" Rachel's eyes lit up. "Yes, I want to come, and I'll stay overnight. May I bring my friend Mary?"

"Sure," I replied. "And, yes, there will be champagne."

It had been Archie's idea to host a party, and I was getting excited about it. Nothing big, we'd invited about ten people, a few from Archie's school, Margie and her fiancé—we'd got to know each other better after Robin's death—Rachel and her friend, oh and John, unfortunately.

"What will I wear?" Rachel asked excitedly. "I'll have to go shopping!"

"You know what? Let's close early and go shopping in Elmville," I suggested.

"Okay, let's go!" Rachel exclaimed. "I'm taking off my bonnet too!" She unpinned it and her long hair spilled out, tumbling around her shoulders.

. . .

New Year's Eve was a twinkle of shiny lights, warm house, and the foggy glow only too many glasses of champagne can induce. I topped off my glass and snagged a piece of cheese from the large charcuterie board on our kitchen island.

Archie and his work friends were sitting in the dining room, all laughing about some crazy school story that you must have had to have been there to enjoy because I didn't find many of their stories to be terribly amusing, although Margie and her fiancé, Doug, seemed entertained, too. I let them enjoy their stories and moved on to the living room. In there, Rachel and Mary sat on the sofa and Nathaniel, the college age son of one of the couples Archie invited, was in the chair next to them, playing a board game, but in my fuzzy state, I didn't know which one. Rachel looked very happy in her sparkly silver dress and her hair hanging long down her back. She also appeared to really enjoy looking at cute Nathaniel. Ah, young love.

John and Debra had left early since Debra got a migraine. I had stumbled back to the kitchen to retrieve another piece of cheese when the doorbell rang. I went to the front door and opened it. John was standing there.

"I thought you left," I said, staring at him.

"I did, but I'm back," he replied. His lips curved into an odd smile. "It's not quite New Year yet."

"Yeah," I said, turning back into the house. John grabbed my arm. "Hey." I snatched it back.

"Oh, sorry, you seem a little off balance," he said.

I rolled my eyes but stumbled over something. John steadied me and led me outside, closing the door behind him. The gust of cold air alerted me, chilling me through the thin red V-neck sweater dress I wore. I turned to go back inside, but John blocked my entry.

"I've been waiting to tell you this, but you're never alone," he hissed. "Always Archie or that Amish girl hanging around."

"What?" I snapped. "Get out of my way, John."

He didn't budge. He put his hands on either side of my face and stared into my eyes. A deep, disturbing stare. "I saw you. I know what you did."

I dodged right, but his hands dropped from my face to my arms. He held me tight. I couldn't move.

"What the fuck, John." I struggled. "Let me go, you freak."

"That's what you always thought about me, wasn't it? What you told Robin about me. That's why she didn't like me anymore and didn't want to go out with me," he bellowed. "It was *you!*"

"No, she just didn't like you!" I screamed, hoping someone inside would hear.

He put his hand over my mouth and hissed again, this time into my ear. "I know what you did, but I don't know why. You were at Robin's that night she died. You killed her."

I vigorously shook my head. He released his hand. "No, I stopped by earlier, and she was fine. I told the cops that. It's not a secret."

"Not then, later," he said.

"I wasn't there later," I replied. I glared at him. "Where were *you*? Watching her? Maybe you killed her. You knew about her nut allergy. And she didn't want you."

"Because of you!" he growled.

Goosebumps flooded my skin, partly because of the cold, partly because John was scaring the hell out of me. *How do I get away from him?*

The front door opened. Archie was standing there, looking confused. *Oh, thank goodness.* I broke away and ran into the warm house.

"Archie, John was just about to leave," I said in a loud voice. "Goodnight, *John!*"

I slammed the door in his face.

. . .

I woke up in my warm bed, Archie slightly snoring beside me. I got up, went to the bathroom, brushed my teeth and pulled my pink terrycloth bathrobe on over my light green cotton pajamas, then padded downstairs. Surprisingly, the kitchen was in neat order. All debris had been thrown out, dishes humming in the dishwasher, counters wiped clean. Fresh coffee sat in a pot, waiting for me. Sweet, sweet Rachel.

She walked out from the living room, also in a bathrobe wrapped around pajamas, holding a mug of coffee.

"Good morning, Aimee." She smiled. "Thought I'd tidy up a bit."

"Thank you so much," I said, pouring a mug of coffee. "It was a nice surprise."

"Thank you for inviting me to your party," she said. "I had so much fun. So did Mary."

"Good. It looked like you talked to Nathaniel quite a bit," I remarked.

She blushed. "Yes, he's going to call me sometime."

"Wow, that's great," I said.

I was glad she'd had a good time, but I had bigger issues.

John.

The freak.

Last night after I slammed the door in his face, Archie went back to his group in the dining room and I stood by the side window, in the foyer, after locking the door, and watched John as he walked to his car and drove out the lane.

What the hell was all that about last night?

He thought I had something to do with Robin's death. Was he out of his mind?

He never answered my question. Where was he when he supposedly saw me go to Robin's house? Along the road, in the field, maybe hiding in the house?

The image of the bag of dates popped into my mind.

The bag inside Robin's refrigerator.

Maybe I had been wrong all along with my guess of who was sending me gifts and other randoms. Maybe this was a person with a secret connection to Listening Lark who had been hiding in plain sight.

FORTY

2024

Aimee

January moved in and the snow continued to fall. Archie had another snow day and was in the dining room doing a virtual school day. I glanced at the clock. Two more hours until he finished for the day.

I sat in the office, looking over our bank accounts. Everything in the accounts looked okay, but I couldn't see the link to our investment account, and I tried to remember if it was on here the last time I checked the accounts. Maybe the bank was updating information and it would be up later. I made a mental note to check.

I leaned back in the office chair and logged out of the bank website. Archie's voice carried over, talking about condensation and the water cycle to his class. My thoughts wandered.

I hadn't seen John since New Year and I hadn't wanted to, but I did have to deal with this problem. I hadn't told Archie about what happened. I wanted to, but hesitated. Was John the one with a connection to Listening Lark? I'd gone over this a million times in my head, but I couldn't see how it was possible.

Problem was, I wasn't sure, and I didn't want to risk Archie learning anything about my past.

When I thought about the facts, I felt the only idea that made sense was John, being the creepy loser that he was, still mourning Robin, more the fantasy of what he thought he could have with her, even though it would never have happened, wanted someone to project that blame onto... me.

People do all sorts of crazy things, even make up stories in their minds, to validate a situation. Who knew what was going on in John's mixed-up mind? His delusion about Robin had him thinking in all kinds of unrealistic directions, and I was an easy target to lash out on, a newcomer to this tight-knit community. As friendly as everyone had been, the newcomers were always suspected when something went awry. I had to just look at the facts as they presented themselves. The facts everyone was aware of at that time. Robin's death was ruled accidental. There was no murder.

What should I do? I was going to see John eventually. Would it be better to wait until that happened or confront him first?

Confrontation seemed a better choice.

I parked my car in the driveway, grabbed my bag in the passenger seat, and walked up the sidewalk to ring the doorbell. The grapevine wreath still hung on the cranberry-colored front door, now with ice and a dusting of snow intertwined with the brown vines.

"Oh, hello, Aimee," Debra greeted when she opened the door. "Good to see you."

"Hi, Debra," I said. "I have way too many strawberry jams. I thought you might like a couple. John mentioned how much you like it on your toast."

"That's so thoughtful," said Debra. She waved me inside. "Come in, would you like some coffee or tea?"

"Coffee would be great." I followed her into the kitchen and placed the bag of jams on the tidy counter.

"Johnny will be out soon," she said, pouring the coffee.

"Okay." I took the coffee and sipped it.

"How have you been, Aimee?" Debra asked. "Come sit at the table with me."

I did and we chatted for a few minutes. Debra told me she'd celebrated her sixty-seventh birthday last week.

"You look great," I remarked. "Definitely not sixty-seven."

"Thank you, good genes run in the family, I guess," she replied.

Those genes must have skipped John. I enjoyed speaking to Debra; she was such a warm interesting person. Her inviting personality reminded me of Aunt Lou in a way. She cared very much about other people and did all she could to help. That's a rarity in this world.

"Grandma." John walked into the kitchen wearing sweat-pants and a sweatshirt. He stopped. "Aimee."

"Hi, Johnny, Aimee was nice enough to bring over some strawberry jam for us." Debra smiled at her grandson.

"How kind," he replied, eyeing the jam. He walked over to the coffeepot and poured a cup.

"Aimee, I'm so sorry. I must get ready for a doctor appoint-ment and haven't had my shower yet. Please stay and visit with Johnny," Debra said, standing up. She gave me a brief hug. "So wonderful to see you."

"Good to see you too," I replied as she walked back the hallway.

John and I sat in silence until we heard the shower turn on. He looked at me.

"I owe you an apology, Aimee," he said. "I'm sorry."

"Thank you," I replied. His words shocked me. I hadn't expected an apology from him, but I would accept it.

"I miss Robin so much, and I get kind of crazy thinking about what happened. I did see you there though."

"Yes, I was there, and I told the police as much," I replied. "That's not a secret."

He nodded. "Did you tell Archie? About what I said?"

I shook my head.

"Really, why?"

"I wasn't sure how to handle it," I said. "He values your friendship. If I tell him, I doubt he would be friends with you."

"Thank you, I value him too." John sighed.

"I accept your apology," I said.

"So, we're okay?" he asked.

"Sure." I stood up and walked to the front door. I turned to him. "Don't ever let something like that happen again though. Enjoy the jam."

He didn't say anything, but I felt him watching me as I walked to the driveway and got into my car. I backed out of the driveway and glanced back.

He was still watching.

FORTY-ONE

2017

The Commune

Dream

We sat under a grove of orange and lemon trees just beyond the Zen Yoga Deck where we did our morning stretches. Only three of us lounged under the green, leafy canopy of lush fruit; the rest of the group went back to the house.

Sun filtered through the leaves making dancing shadows we laughed at as we smoked the sacred herb, inhaling its anxiety-reducing properties. I, for one, needed the calming element and indulged in its haze wholeheartedly. A slight chill lingered in the air, typical of a winter morning, even in California, although our bodies were still warmed by our intense yoga workout. My heart thumped loudly in my chest, although that might have been for other reasons.

"How long have you taught yoga?" Sunny asked Venus, her long legs stretched out next to me. Venus sat across from us, in a short white gown, the same as Sunny wore. I had on my comfortable cotton shorts and a tank top. We practiced yoga nude, but some clothes were needed afterward in the early morning crispness.

"Two years," said Venus, her voice throaty. Long dark hair spilled down her slim shoulders. "I learned when I was seventeen."

"And you're nineteen now, right?" Sunny said. "That's how old I was when I met Dream and joined Listening Lark. I'm twenty-one now."

Venus nodded, looking at me through her long eyelashes. I could have her if I wanted. I knew I could. And I really wanted to; it was all I'd thought about lately. This desire for her was killing me. She consumed my thoughts. Her lips, her breasts, how she would feel. She intoxicated me.

"Cool, yeah, I needed something different in my life, something to belong to. My mom died recently, and I've been dealing with that," she said. "Listening Lark feels right to me."

"We're so glad you're here," I said. "Sorry about your mom."

She nodded. "What is great about this place is that we live in the here and now, right? Right now, I'm under some beautiful trees with some beautiful people and I feel so happy."

We all smiled and looked at each other. Belonging to a group like Listening Lark gave us a close bond. Individuals functioning as one unit. I'd always loved that theory. I looked at Sunny, relaxed and leaning against me, enjoying Venus's company as much as me. A thought crossed my mind. A thought I'd been having all week. Could it be possible? Maybe we could be a throuple? Maybe Sunny would be into it. She always said it was only me and her, that she didn't share. But maybe she'd make an exception for Venus? I mean, look at her! My mind raced now. *How could I make this happen for us?*

"Venus!" a voice called. We looked to see Willow standing in the yard. "Can I talk to you for a minute?"

"Sure." Venus got up and walked over to Willow. They disappeared from our sight.

"She's great," I remarked, watching her walk away.

"Venus, yeah she is," Sunny said.

She stood up to pick an orange off the tree. She peeled it.

I stood too and leaned down to kiss her. "Not as great as you."

"Of course not." She laughed. She fed me a segment of orange and ate one herself.

"I love you," I whispered to her. And I did.

"I love you too."

"Our love is strong, isn't it?" I asked.

She nodded and kissed me, deeper this time. I pulled her close to me, my hands running down her back, and we continued to kiss. She dropped the orange.

I heard a twig snap and looked up. Venus walked toward us. Our gazes met and we stared at one another for a moment. She took off the short gown she was wearing and tossed it to the ground. She was completely naked and walking directly to us. Was this really happening, or an unbelievable dream?

I continued to kiss Sunny, my eyes on Venus, and motioned to her to come closer. My gaze drank in her body. I'd seen it before, but now, it was obvious she was presenting it just for me, for us.

Venus stood close behind Sunny, and I lifted my hand from Sunny to touch Venus's breast, while still kissing Sunny. My eyes locked with Venus. I was going to try this. My heart pounded and other regions did too.

Venus moved closer, and I lifted my lips from Sunny, my other hand still on her. I kissed Venus.

Sunny's eyes flew open.

She jerked away.

"What the hell? What are you doing?" she demanded.

"Please, Sunny," I pleaded. "Let's try this. You, me and Venus. We would be so good together."

She pointed a finger at me. "I told you that I don't share. I'll never share you!"

"I know, but I really want this," I said, staring at her. "It will be good for our relationship."

"You are fucking insane!" she yelled and ran away across the yard.

"I'm sorry," I said to Venus. I ran after Sunny.

I reached the guesthouse and turned the knob. It was locked. We never locked it; I didn't even know it had a lock.

"Sunny, let me in," I called. I pulled harder on the knob.

"Go away!" she screamed.

"Please... I'm sorry."

No response. I tried to get her to open the door, but only silence met me on the other side. Adrenaline coursed through me. She couldn't lock *me* out! I pounded on the door, but she didn't answer.

"Sunny, open the damn door!" I yelled, punching the door. Over and over again.

"I said *go away*!"

I stood still for a moment doing some deep breathing. My hand ached and bled from its impact to the door. "Calmness and balance." I whispered to myself. "Calmness and balance."

I went away.

FORTY-TWO

2024

Aimee

My jewelry making was pretty much a disaster. I didn't have the creative skill, or patience, for it. So, I gave up and started sketching instead. I liked doing pencil drawings, rather than color, because I enjoyed their simplicity. It was the perfect hobby for a snowy January.

Sketching also gave me peace. My mind had been going in a million directions lately. Nothing in my life was stable, as always, but in a constant state of unrest. My time with Dream at the commune was ironically probably the most stable time of my life.

At least things with John were at a standstill. I didn't like him or trust him, but if he left me alone, fine. I wished I could cut off his friendship with Archie, but I didn't know how. I still wondered if Dream was lurking around or if John had some connection to Listening Lark and was the one sending the strange gifts; but I couldn't figure out how he would have such an intimate knowledge of my relationship with Dream. None of it made sense. How would he know about those personal things? Only Dream would know. But what did he want? Why drag it out like this? I wished he would just show up in person and get it over with; although as much as I wanted that, I felt sick at the prospect, and weirdly excited.

Archie was acting strange too. Standoffish, unlike him, and distant. I didn't know why, but wondered if he could sense I was keeping secrets from him. I didn't want to dredge up old memories from the past. What would he think of me?

I picked up my sketch book lying on the nightstand and walked over to my jewelry box. I lifted the top and stared at the gold locket found in my underwear drawer on Christmas morning. My thoughts traveled back to the other gold locket.

My heart hurt thinking about the intense love I'd had for Dream, different than I had with Archie. With Dream, it was as if we existed on another level of consciousness, the love fortifying every step of our day. Consuming. Intoxicating. Maybe even a little obsessive. Our craving to be with each other was our main purpose in life.

Until it wasn't.

Over those three years, after Listening Lark, when I languished in Aunt Lou's house sunk in such sadness, I played my days, our days, at Listening Lark over and over in my mind. Such contrasts, of sunshine and darkness, that in the end swirled together until everything broke apart. Part of me felt guilty because Archie and I didn't have that sort of love, where you can feel it in your very core; but I was certain I'd never experience that kind of love again in my lifetime. My love for Archie was real, but it was steady and predictable. I guess it was an adult love. Not that what I had with Dream wasn't real, but it certainly wasn't based in reality. The whole Listening Lark idea wasn't based in reality, but it existed. And when it was good, it was so good, all you could ever want. If I had the chance to go back to that time in my life and spend one day in that guesthouse with Dream before everything went wrong, I would do it in an instant. Even now, thinking about it, I don't know how everything went so badly, so quickly.

How do you love someone so deeply and hate them too? How do you miss someone but never want to see them again? As much as I wished them gone, my feelings, and love, for Dream would never die.

And secretly, I hoped he was back.

The Winter Carnival at Poplin Elementary School was a big event. The gym, filled with various stands, coin toss games, dart games, guessing games, basketball games, basically, many games, plus a face painting booth and photo booth.

Outside the gym, in the cafeteria, were food stands. Typically, goodies like hot dogs, hamburgers, French fries, funnel cakes, and milkshakes. The PTA had a bake sale with various homemade offerings, including my cream cheese brownies.

Archie and I manned the photo booth. There were two sections to it, one an old-fashioned photo booth where you could pay a dollar for a strip of three pictures. And the second part was a designated area where people could take selfies in front of different backgrounds, like an ocean scene, a NYC street, and a scene in front of Poplin Elementary School. The selfie backgrounds were free and most popular. Children and adults both swarmed the various scenes to take a picture.

"Two for the photo booth, please," a little girl requested. I grinned and took her money. She went into the booth with her friend.

"Make sure to smile, Clara!" Archie said.

"Okay, Mr. Greencastle!" The girl giggled.

"One of your students?" I asked.

"Maybe next year. She's in second grade. Her sister, Leigh, is in my class this year," he replied.

"Hey, let's take a selfie," I suggested, grabbing my phone.

Archie grabbed my hand. "Okay, NYC, ocean or school?"

"All of them!"

We posed at each background, smiling, then pulling surprise faces, then silly faces. We laughed with each pose and scrolled through the pictures on my phone together.

"Oh, that's a good one." Archie pointed to one of the NYC shots. "Send that one to me. I'm putting it in my classroom."

"Mr. Greencastle!" A group of third-grade girls came over to our booth. "Will you take our picture?"

"Okay." He took one of the girls' phones. "You know this is a selfie station, right?"

"We know! We're taking more than one picture. The rest will be selfies. And take a selfie with all of us, you too!"

"Okay." He laughed and took the picture. "Me too?"

"Yes!" the girls said in unison.

I laughed and went back to the photo booth where a line was forming. I took the money and the line moved along.

"Hey, Aimee," a voice said.

I looked up from the cash box and Margie stood in front of me. "Hi, Margie, good to see you!"

"Thank you again for inviting us to your New Year's Eve party. We had so much fun." She smiled.

"I'm so glad," I replied. "Are you doing the photo booth?"

"We were, but Doug got distracted by something," she said. "But that's okay. I want to talk to you about something anyway."

"Okay, um... do you want to talk now?"

"Probably nothing, but I wanted to mention it to you. Robin told you how weird John was when I wouldn't go out with him, right? This was before I was seeing Doug."

"She did." I nodded. "She said he was... kind of stalking you?"

"Yes, it seemed like that, until I started dating Doug," Margie said. "Anyway, I was driving past your house a few times the last couple of weeks. My aunt lives out your way. Last week, I noticed John's truck parked on the dirt lane down the road from you, and he was walking out of the small woods across from your house."

"Okay." I stared at her.

"Then this week, I saw the truck again, parked in that dirt lane. I drove very slowly past the woods. He was in the trees, crouched down, and I swear he had binoculars pointed toward your house."

"Really?" I raised my eyebrows. Anger flickered inside me. *This guy doesn't stop.* "That is strange."

"I thought so and that's why I wanted to tell you. Maybe it's nothing, I hope it's nothing. At first, I thought he might be hunting rabbits, which he sometimes does there. That's Robin's parents' land and they don't mind if he hunts there, but I don't think he had a rifle."

"Hmmm. I'm glad you told me," I said. "I really appreciate it and if you see anything else odd, please let me know."

"Most definitely." Margie looked around. "Now I just need to find Doug. He's probably by the funnel cake stand."

I lay on the sofa flicking through Netflix and found nothing I was interested in watching, despite the many, many choices. Archie was at school today and I felt lazy. Honestly, I'd barely got out of bed the last few days. Maybe having a few months off from the store wasn't a good idea for me. Some of those old feelings resurfaced for me, and I did not want to be pulled down to a state where I couldn't even rise in the morning. I needed to make an appointment with my psychiatrist in Philly and perhaps get back on the medicine that helped me clear the chaos in my brain. Things had been good for the last few years, and I'd stopped taking it. My life was such a whirlwind for a while, especially after meeting Archie, then Aunt Lou's death, getting married, buying our little farm, and settling in Poplin.

But now things had slowed. I had too much time on my hands. And too many worries.

I'd told Archie what Margie said about John, and he'd brushed it off. Shouldn't he be concerned about this odd friend of his? How did he not see John's strangeness? He should always take my side. I was his wife! Anger surged through me thinking about it now.

This perfect life I thought we were creating in Poplin suddenly didn't feel so perfect anymore. Had I just been caught up in the idea of it? I thought this would be my second chance at happiness and I was happy, for a time. But I still held the hope of being happy again. I felt so out of sorts. I needed to focus on the facts. Those facts being John sneaking around in the woods across the road. What did he think he was going to see with his binoculars? It was a cold January with snow on the ground. The only time we were outside was to feed the chickens, walk to the car or shovel snow. Or was he waiting for the house to be empty, so that he could leave another unsettling gift for me?

I picked up my phone and called Dr. Daly. I needed to get back to feeling good, mentally, and physically, to stay on top of things.

FORTY-THREE

2017

The Commune
Dream

Sunny didn't talk to me for three excruciating days. She kept the door to the guesthouse locked when she was inside and locked the door when she left, usually to go talk to Raindrop. I tried numerous times to talk to her, but she ignored me as if I didn't exist to her. I was sure she hated me.

I mostly hung out by the pool, hoping to get a chance to talk to her. Venus kept her distance, and then she and Willow went to stay at Grandmother's house for a few days, to help Moonbeam and Lilac with some new jewelry ideas since they were expanding on their creations. It was good to have distance from her as I sorted things out with Sunny.

Now it was evening, probably after eleven because everyone had gone to bed, and I lay on the cushioned lounge chair just outside the guesthouse door at the side of the shimmering pool. The lamp by the front window was on and Sunny was inside, probably asleep.

I couldn't sleep, like the previous two nights. Sure, I'd get a few hours of rest here and there, but not much. I was an idiot. I knew what Sunny's reaction would be, but I still tried. She was never going to forgive me.

I stared at the half-moon above me, enjoying the quiet of the evening, but this wasn't where I wanted to be. I wanted to be with her. I wanted to be inside that guesthouse, in bed with the woman I loved—the woman I would always love. I'd never felt like that with anyone else in my life, and I had completely screwed it up. Sunny and I were meant for one another. We were a team. Partners in everything. I never even told her what I was thinking about Venus. Maybe if I had, things would have been different.

The guesthouse door opened. Sunny stood in the doorway staring at me. She walked away but left the door ajar. I hurried over and walked inside.

"You unlocked the door," I said, meeting her gaze.

"Yes."

I moved closer to her. Her hair was damp and fresh smelling. She must have just taken a shower. "I missed you."

"Did you?" she asked, a quick glare darted at me. "What about Venus?"

"I'm sorry," I said, never dropping her gaze. "I'm stupid. I'm so stupid. Please forgive me."

"Hmmm..." She moved closer to me. "You are stupid."

I nodded.

"And I missed you too," she said. Her lips hovered by mine. I kissed her softly. She responded, leaning into me. A few tears escaped my eyes.

"Thank you for forgiving me," I said, wiping them away.

"Are you crying?"

"No. Maybe." I kissed her again. "I promise no secrets between us ever. We tell each other everything."

"Everything," she agreed.

I kissed her neck, her breasts, and down her flat stomach.

She laughed because her stomach was always ticklish. She pulled me back up to her, grabbed my hands, and led us to our bed.

The week flew by and now we helped Brother Jim move himself and the other family members into Listening Lark's new home next door. River and Branch would stay at Grandmother's house to work on the winery we planned to start up; I'd be overseeing the enterprise, something new that I was excited about doing for Listening Lark. Branch's family had a large winery in Napa, and he knew quite a bit about the business. Learning the winery process would be interesting to me and it felt like everything was falling into place in so many aspects of my life.

Sunny and I fell back into our normal routine, and it felt so good. Things seemed to calm with Raindrop too. Life with Sunny in the guesthouse was exactly what I wanted. *How could I want more?*

We still did yoga with Venus and the others in the morning. We had some conversations with Venus about the new house and topics of that nature. A bit awkward in the beginning, but things smoothed out quickly. Everything was fine between the three of us. I think everyone moved on from the incident.

My peacefulness returned. Sunny and I would always be together.

FORTY-FOUR

2024

Aimee

Dr. Daly's office was an oasis of calm in busy downtown Center City. Pale pink walls blending with crisp white furniture, soft floral pillows in a delicate pattern on her comfortable sofa and equally comfortable overstuffed chairs. A long, slim coffee table in front of the sofa had a box of tissues on it and an etched glass candy bowl filled with Hershey's Kisses. The lighting was dimmed, with a warm floral lamp lit on a side table next to the sofa. I'd spent many hours in this room. Many hours trying to heal my mind and move on from the trauma of my past.

"Aimee," Dr. Hazel Daly said. She sat in one of the overstuffed chairs with her notebook and pen at the ready. Her laptop sat on the coffee table. "It's been a long time."

"Yes," I said.

"How have you been?"

"Not good. Not terrible, but I'm having some trouble."

"What kind of trouble?"

"Getting motivated, sometimes getting out of bed in the morning. I think I need to start medication again."

Dr. Daly nodded. "Yes, that is something we could do, though I think we should talk first. I'm glad you recognized the issue and came to see me. We should keep regular appointments."

"I think so too."

"How about everything else? Have the nightmares returned?"

"No, but..."

"Yes?"

"I've been thinking about them lately. My parents."

"Okay, what about?"

I fiddled with the edge of the floral pillow. "Maybe I could have done something differently. You know how I play out the entire scenario in my mind. Was I wrong by doing what I did?"

Dr. Daly paused. "It's a complicated situation, Aimee, and you were only seventeen. It's easy to have hindsight now and think of other options, but in the heat of the moment you did what you thought was right at the time."

I nodded. I'd forgotten how much I liked Dr. Daly. She validated my feelings and helped me put things into perspective.

But Dr. Daly didn't know all my secrets, only a few.

FORTY-FIVE

2013

Aimee

The rain fell steadily in the morning giving our already gloomy house a deeper level of darkness. I lay on the living room sofa, flicking through the TV channels with the remote, but finding nothing of interest.

I heard her fumbling around in the back bedroom. The shower ran and then the hair dryer. Mixed feelings swelled inside me. Glad she was finally moving around. She hadn't left her bedroom in two days, a common occurrence lately, but now I'd have to deal with her and that was always so exhausting.

The door creaked open, and Mom walked out. She wore jeans that hung loose on her ever-thinning frame and a plain white sweatshirt. Her hair was washed and brushed. She even wore makeup. She looked good, better than she had in weeks.

"Mom," I said, jumping off the sofa. "You look nice."

She shrugged, giving me the minimal response I was accustomed to receiving over the last few months. She walked out to the kitchen, opened the refrigerator, and poured a glass of orange juice.

I walked over to her. "Are we going somewhere? Let me change, it'll only take a minute."

Mom laughed. "I'm going somewhere, but you're not coming."

This shit again. She would never forgive me. What I did was for her. Why couldn't she see that?

"Really?" I sharpened my tone. "Why are you still treating me like this? It's been months! Why won't you understand?"

Mom glared at me. "I understand that you took him from me, and I'll never forgive you for it."

Tears rose inside me and I ran to my bedroom. I would not allow her to see me cry. Never again. I stayed there for a few hours, having fallen asleep on my bed. Groggy, I got up and made my way to the kitchen. I poured a glass of juice just as my mother had done earlier in the day.

I noticed a piece of paper lying on the kitchen counter and picked it up. Aunt Lou's name and phone number were scrawled across it in my mother's handwriting.

Weird.

One hour later, the phone rang.

My mother was dead.

FORTY-SIX
2024

Aimee

I sat at one of the windows in our bedroom, the one at the front of the house. I kept the blackout curtains mostly closed, except a small middle section where I watched across the road with my binoculars. It was a fair distance away, but as I zoomed in my focus, I was surprised at my clear and close view of the small woods across the road.

John could see more than I realized if he was watching our house from that vantage point. I'd better make sure to keep the curtains closed. I continued to sit there, on a soft cushioned ottoman, at random times throughout the day, hoping to spot John on one of his excursions. No luck yet.

I felt better today. The medication Dr. Daly prescribed last week was kicking in and some of the edginess I'd experienced was tapering off. I'd made another appointment with her for next week and looked forward to it. I held the binoculars up. There was movement across the snow-covered field. A man in camouflage coveralls walked toward the woods. No vehicle in sight, so he must have parked in the dirt lane down the road. He walked in a familiar way.

John.

I watched him with the binoculars, zooming in on him. He walked into the woods, far enough among the trees to be unseen from the road. He took off his backpack, sat it on the ground, unzipped it and lifted out binoculars. He turned and faced toward our house, lifting the binoculars.

I backed up, the closeness of his image jolting me. I stood back a discreet distance in a dark room watching the stalker search for a glimpse of me.

The cold air whipped around us as we drove the new side-by-side ATV through the deserted fields. It was a two-seater in electric blue and we were having a ton of fun zipping around our land in it. Archie had a good idea with this one. Asking John to join us on his four-wheeler, not so much.

I pulled my hat down further past my ears. I wore warm winter coveralls, thick gloves, and dark sunglasses. The brightness of the snow and sunshine was blinding, more so than a hot, sunny summer day.

Archie floored the ATV. We sped across the frozen back field around the creek at the bottom and back up over the slight hill to the flat area. Ahead of us, John was flying on his red four-wheeler, tossing up snow in our path.

John's strangeness with me had continued, and Archie still claimed not to notice anything off about him. I thought of all the people who'd noticed John's behavior as being abnormal—Robin, Margie, Rachel, even Rachel's mother all felt the same as me—yet how did this not register with Archie? Was he so desperate for a friend that he would ignore something that impacted his wife? Maybe he just needed to find another friend and then John wouldn't be so important to him. Maybe Doug, Margie's fiancé, would be a possibility.

"This is fun, isn't it?" Archie yelled over the hum of the engine. A few snow flurries spun in the air around us. "Even in the cold."

"It is, but I'm ready to go in and get warm by a fire."

Hot chocolate, a warm fire, and snuggling under a fuzzy blanket sounded like heaven to me right now. It was fun, but my fingers were becoming numb, even protected by thick gloves.

"Okay." He turned around and headed back to the house. John followed us and we parked the vehicles by the side of the garage.

"Let John go home. I don't want him coming inside," I told Archie.

"Why?"

I smiled and rolled my eyes. *You know why. Oh, he likes to play these games.* "I want to be alone with you."

He laughed. "You just don't want him around, but that's okay. I want to be alone with you too. And maybe we'll take this out later today by ourselves."

"Maybe, if you're lucky."

He grinned. "I'm already lucky because I'm here with you."

I laughed.

Maybe Archie was finally figuring it out and taking the right side. His wife's.

FORTY-SEVEN
2017

The Commune
Dream

Anger flooded through me, and I stormed out of the guesthouse, leaving Sunny crying on the floor. I paced around the pool several times, then walked into the yard to the yoga deck and paced that space, feeling anything but Zen. Frustration and irritation rose inside me, and I hated feeling that way. I didn't like myself in that state. Why was Sunny doing this to me, to us? She'd started having private talks with Raindrop again; maybe they had never stopped, and I hadn't noticed, but things were changing now because of those secret meetings. Things that involved me and her. If she would just let everything alone, we wouldn't have the problems we now faced.

Raindrop's ex-husband was a prominent LA attorney. She'd spoken to him about Jim Bob, the abuse, and the commune. He filed a restraining order stating Brother Jim must stay fifty yards away from her and her property. In addition, she wanted all members of Listening Lark out of her home, except River, who was leaving the family and staying with Raindrop. We had to move out tomorrow. *Tomorrow!*

I stomped over to the property next door, now owned by us. Technically Fire owned it, but he was a family member. What one owned, we all enjoyed, was the motto of Listening Lark. Sharing as one created unity in all. Too bad Sunny didn't seem to adhere to this concept. Now that we were thrown out of the guesthouse, would we move here or back to Grandmother's house? Nobody was outside and I was glad. I wasn't in the mood to talk to anyone. I sat on the grass next to the swing set and sighed.

What happened to being partners, not keeping any secrets from one another? This was one hell of a secret she'd kept from me! Why wouldn't she have talked to me about what was going on before things changed so drastically? Anger burned inside me like it used to many years before. I was so damn angry! I punched the ground next to me. And again. And again, until my hand was dirty with soil and grass. Breathing exercises weren't going to help me today. I wanted to hurt something.

Or someone.

The sliding glass door opened and Jim Bob stepped out onto the patio. He was wearing a white bathrobe and holding a blue coffee mug.

"Dream," he said. "I guess you heard the news."

"Yeah, guess I'm moving," I muttered. "Thanks to Sunny."

"Sunny?"

"Yeah, I think she talked Raindrop into all of this."

Jim Bob frowned. "Why would she do that?"

"I don't know," I said. "I don't know if I can trust her anymore."

We took the master bedroom at Grandmother's house. Jim Bob thought it was best, since I would be overseeing the winery, and would be in charge here, as much as I wanted to be. I didn't have a preference; that bedroom or the cabin was fine with me. I didn't want either; I wanted the guesthouse at Raindrop's house, but that was over, thanks to Sunny. I was still angry at her, and she didn't understand why I was so angry. Getting us thrown out of the guesthouse was one thing, but then cops showed up yesterday because of a fight Raindrop had with Brother Jim the night before. Sunny had called them! The cops. After I'd begged her not to.

She knew that was a risk for me, but she didn't seem to care. Was she trying to get back at me for what I'd tried with Venus? Well she'd gone way over the line this time. Way too far.

As pissed off as I was about moving out of the guesthouse, part of me was relieved to move back into Grandmother's house. I could relax there and get myself back to a peaceful state. In all the chaos, I'd allowed the anger to take me over. I was so consumed by it and it felt justified to me, but I didn't want to live with that type of seething inside me. I wanted calm; I sought balance and I'd regain it. At least I wouldn't have cops there. Whatever mess erupted between Raindrop and Jim Bob did not involve me.

Would Sunny and I last? I wasn't sure now.

FORTY-EIGHT

2024

Aimee

I pulled on a T-shirt and soft cotton lounge pants. I walked over to my jewelry box and opened it. I lifted out the turquoise necklace I'd bought the first time I'd met Dream.

I stared at myself in the mirror, fingering the necklace. My hair was darker, as it usually was during the cold East Coast winter months, and there were a few wrinkles I hadn't noticed before on my face. I'd thought a lot about Dream lately and the events leading to the end.

Venus.

He knew I would never go for a throuple. He *knew* that.

But I forgave him. Why couldn't he forgive me?

He didn't know my past, but I had to help Raindrop get away from Brother Jim. The way Dream flipped out about that and the night the cops showed up had shocked me. He was so angry with me, but cryptic about his past. How was I supposed to know calling the cops could have put him in danger? What did he do? I still didn't know. Raindrop had told me once that Jim Bob had hinted Dream's anger had gotten him in trouble with women in the past. That's why he had to avoid the police. I had my suspicions, but I never found out the entire truth.

The day we left the guesthouse, I went to say goodbye to Raindrop and return the key she'd given me earlier.

"Keep it," she said. "You can stay in the guesthouse anytime, but not Dream. I like him, but he's more like Brother Jim than you realize."

I thanked her and we left to move into his grandmother's house. I remembered leaving the guesthouse and feeling a sense of melancholy that I didn't understand at the time. It was only later I knew what it meant.

It was the last place that Dream and I were happy together.

I stirred the chicken noodle soup and looked up when the side door opened in the mud room. I heard Archie as he removed his boots and hung up his coat. A few minutes later he came into the kitchen, snowflakes still in his hair.

He walked over and kissed me. His gaze went to the turquoise necklace around my neck.

"New necklace?" he commented. "I don't remember seeing it before."

"No, an old one." I turned back to the soup.

"Oh." I felt him stare at me for a moment. I glanced at him, meeting his gaze. He went to the refrigerator and pulled out a bottle of water. "John's going to stop by soon. He's taking me rabbit hunting with him."

"What?" I dropped the spoon on the counter. "You don't hunt."

"No, I'm just going to walk along," he said.

"Where?"

"Over at the farm where Angela was murdered, actually," he said.

"Doesn't that creep you out?"

"Not really. They arrested that guy."

We'd heard last week that the married man had had a hole in his alibi and lied about seeing Angela the day she was murdered.

"Hmmm... you want to be around John with a hunting rifle," I remarked. "I told you I saw him in the trees across the road watching our house. You really don't find that strange behavior?"

"It is," he agreed. "But maybe I can find out what's going on with him."

"Sure, maybe," I said, going back to stirring the soup.

What are you up to, Archie?

FORTY-NINE
2017

The Commune
Dream

I turned over in bed, now lying flat on my back, still staring at the ceiling fan going around above me. I pulled up the covers and sighed. Sunny had gotten up early to work in the garden, but I wanted to sleep in today. Unfortunately, sleep eluded me. I think Sunny just wanted to avoid me, as she had ever since we'd moved in here. I heard the shower in the hall bathroom turn off and wondered who else was up early.

I closed my eyes and tried to fall back to sleep. Sunny and I were barely talking. Last night was nothing but arguing. I'd been sure we'd work it out, but right now, I was still angry with her, despite my efforts to enter a state of peacefulness. And she didn't understand why I was so mad. To her, it wasn't a big deal, which made me angrier.

My bedroom door opened. I opened my eyes. Venus stood in the doorway, wrapped in a red towel. Her hair hung long and wet, fresh from a shower. We stared at each other for a moment, or two. I pulled down the covers. She closed the door and dropped the towel.

"We shouldn't," I said as she joined me in bed. I kissed her and she kissed me back, putting her arms around my neck and her unbelievable body against mine.

"But we want to," she whispered.

Lust took over and before I knew it, Venus was on top of me, the bedcovers now tossed off the bed, and it was awesome. Like I knew it would be with her.

The bedroom door opened. Sunny stood in the doorway for only a moment watching Venus as she moved on top of me, my hands on her hips, our bodies joining in the most intimate of ways. Then, she stared at me, our gaze met, and she ran out of the room.

And I finished.

FIFTY

2024

Aimee

Dr. Daly's sofa was the most comfortable I'd ever encountered. I really should ask her where she bought it. I stared at the antique clock on the wall; she'd had it ever since I started coming here, shortly after my seventeenth birthday.

"How have you been feeling?" Dr. Daly asked, a warm smile directed at me.

"Better. More energy, less edgy," I replied.

"Good. Anything else going on?"

I paused. "I've been thinking a lot about Dream."

"Dream," she repeated. "Was that your boyfriend in California?"

I nodded.

"Things did not end well with him."

"No."

"What have you been thinking about regarding him?"

"Mostly about my feelings for him." My voice cracked and tears welled in my eyes. I took a deep breath and pushed them away.

"Which were what, exactly?" Dr. Daly asked.

"Love, anger, but mostly love. Intense love."

"More intense than the love you now have with your husband?"

I hesitated, pondering the question. The same question I'd been thinking about for some time. "It's different than the love I have with Archie."

"Young love is usually more intense, and all relationships are different. We don't love two different people the same way." Dr. Daly wrote in her notebook.

"I guess that's true."

She watched me. "Your relationship with Dream, was that the first serious relationship you had?"

"Yes."

"Did you share with him about your past trauma?"

"No."

"Have you shared it with Archie?"

I shook my head.

Dr. Daly turned her head and gazed at me. "Why do you think that is?"

"I don't know. It's not something I want to talk about with anyone."

"You talk to me about it."

"That's different. I don't think other people will understand."

"Aimee, it was self-defense. You know that."

"Yes."

"You don't think the men who love, or loved you, would understand what happened?"

I shrugged. "What if they don't really love me?"

I poured another cup of coffee, grabbed my sketchbook and pencils, then sat at the kitchen table. I sketched a barn in a summer landscape. I was getting tired of the cold, snowy weather, so a warm scene appealed to me.

I was in a good mood this morning. Archie had left for school earlier than normal. I hadn't seen him today as my schedule was a bit different, but he texted me before leaving the house. He had some paperwork he wanted to catch up on in his classroom. Now I was enjoying a quiet house and some creative time.

A text popped up on my phone, lying on the table next to me. I glanced at it. Archie. That was odd. He should be in class now.

> Lock all the doors, if you are home. School is in lockdown. There was a shooting not far from the school.

> What??

> Lock all the doors. That's all I know.

Strange. I went to check the doors, windows too. Everything was secure and I continued sketching. Could there have been another murder in Poplin?

The shooting turned out to be a hunter's stray bullet, according to local gossip. John Larabe had been out rabbit hunting when he was hit. Fortunately for him he wore a bullet-proof vest, unusual for a hunter, but John had proved to be an unusual guy many times in the past, so no surprise. What was surprising was that no one came forward to admit they had been hunting nearby and may have discharged the bullet, despite it being an accidental shooting.

"I can't believe it," Archie said, turning off the TV when the local news ended. "It was John. I talked to him and he's okay, but wow."

"Unbelievable," I replied.

"What is going on in this town?" Archie paced the living room.

"I don't know," I agreed. "It's crazy."

Archie frowned and stared at me. "You never liked him."

"What is that supposed to mean?"

Archie shrugged. "I don't know. The whole situation is very odd. First Angela, then Robin, now John gets shot? What the hell is going on?"

"Two were accidents. Angela was the only murder and they've arrested someone for that. Obviously, Poplin is not the quiet, serene community we thought it was."

"Damn right." Archie frowned. "I don't even know if I still want to live here."

I pursed my lips. I wasn't going to argue with him about John and, as for the town, well I was having doubts about staying there too. If we moved, I wondered if I'd continue receiving the strange reminders of the past. Would he follow me wherever I went?

FIFTY-ONE

2024

Aimee

I stopped by Debra's house on my way to the store to drop off a basket of blueberry muffins for her and John. He was recovering from being shot, although he wasn't injured, only bruised and sore, since he had worn the vest. Archie had encouraged me to make the gesture.

I parked my car and walked up the sidewalk to ring the doorbell. Before I could though, the door swung open and Debra stood in the doorway, smiling at me.

"Oh, Aimee!" she greeted. She held a stack of envelopes in her hand. "What a nice surprise. Let me pop these into the mailbox and then we can have some coffee. I just put a fresh pot on!"

"Sure," I said, entering the house. I placed the muffin basket on the table. The aroma of fresh coffee filled the tidy kitchen. The house was quiet except for the hum of a television in the back bedroom. I guessed John was awake. I wouldn't be staying long.

"Aimee, thank you for the muffins," Debra said, smiling at

the basket and then me. "Johnny loves those muffins as much as I do."

"Good, enjoy them," I said. "Just wanted to let you two know Archie and I are thinking about you both after what happened."

"Isn't it terrible?" Debra touched her chest. "If he hadn't been wearing that vest, it would have been so much worse. But my Johnny is a stickler for safety."

"Well, that's good." I smiled at Debra. "I really must go. I have to open the store."

"Come on." Debra was already pouring the coffee into two mugs. "Just one cup."

I nodded. "Okay, just one."

We sat at her kitchen table covered in a cheery yellow table-cloth. I smiled at her. I liked Debra; she reminded me of Aunt Lou, in a way.

"Johnny has a nasty bruise on his chest, but that will heal soon enough. I'm so thankful the Lord was looking out for him. So strange that it was a stray bullet from another hunter. That's what the police think, you know."

"Oh, do they have any idea who fired the shot?"

She shook her head. "No, and nobody came forward, which is strange because it must have been an accident."

I sipped my coffee. "Sure, maybe they think they'd be in trouble though, even if it was accidental."

"Perhaps, well, all I know is I'm going to have one of these muffins right now, and I'm sure Johnny will have one when he wakes up."

"I'm awake, Grandma." John appeared from the hallway into the kitchen. He looked at me. "Hello, Aimee."

"Aimee brought us some muffins. Wasn't that kind of her?"

He grinned. "Very neighborly."

I stood. "Well, I'll leave you two. I have to open the store. Have a great day."

"Bye, Aimee," Debra said. "Thanks again."

"I'll walk you to your car," John said.

"No need," I said quickly.

He stared at me. "No, I want to."

I shrugged my shoulders.

We walked outside the short distance to my car. I turned to say goodbye and John was right behind me, close; his breath smelled like stale coffee, and I could see some brown stains on his teeth from this personal vantage point.

"I know you did it," he hissed at me. "I know who you are."

"Did what?" I tried to push him back, but he didn't budge.

"Don't, Grandma might be watching. I don't want to upset her." He leaned down and whispered in my ear, his stale breath hot against my skin. "I know you shot me."

I glared at him. "You know nothing. It was an accidental shooting. Do you think I was out rabbit hunting?"

He stepped back. "I think you should be careful." Then he turned and walked back to the house.

I looked out the front window. Wind swirled outside, whipping up the loose snow on the six inches or so of the white stuff left from the weekend snowstorm. It seemed to storm more here than in Philly, and it was less than a two-hour trip between them.

The fireplace warmed the living room. I lifted a few logs from the log holder sitting to the side and added them to the crackling fire. I stared as the flames danced and sizzled. Living here wasn't exactly what I had envisioned. Archie had been acting more and more weird lately, and I understood his sentiment about maybe not wanting to live here anymore. Maybe country life wasn't for us. Poplin wasn't what we'd expected; parts were wonderful, but I didn't know if this town was a good fit for us. Everything hit him hard and I'm not sure if this was

my imagination or not, but he wasn't as attentive or even interested in me, like he had been before the New Year. Maybe the
shock of Robin's death and John's shooting so close together was
the reason. Hopefully, we would work through it together. I
would not allow him to close me out. Maybe we should plan a
vacation, somewhere warmer, away from all this snow and cold.
Somewhere by the ocean. Warm sand and cold drinks. Long,
lazy mornings in bed. Yes, I liked that idea.

I sat on the plush patterned carpet in front of the fireplace
and continued to stare at its energy. The movement of fire
always put me into a trancelike state. The flicker, the sparks, the
building heat. Funny, I never saw myself returning to Pennsylvania. I thought I'd stay a Cali girl, but life didn't work out that
way. What we plan isn't always what we do. Or what we get.

What if things had gone differently? Would I still be living
in California with Dream? Would we still be in Listening Lark?
Would we still be in love with each other?

My teapot whistled in the kitchen. I stood and walked into
the kitchen to take it off the stove. I poured the steaming water
into my waiting mug, then returned the kettle to the stove. I
continued to stand, staring at the kettle, but my mind had traveled elsewhere...

Warm sunshine, sparkling blue pool, the scent of sacred
herb hanging heavy in the air, Dream's arm around me, his lips
kissing my own. I couldn't imagine ever experiencing happiness
like I did in that time of my life.

I had thought about Dream so much lately. I shouldn't. I
couldn't. And I was with Archie now. I loved Archie. He was a
good person and a good husband, but it was so different than the
love I had experienced with Dream. I felt my love for Dream in
every fiber of my body. I closed my eyes.

But look how it ended.

Tears sprang in my eyes.

FIFTY-TWO

2017

The Commune

Dream

Sunny packed a bag and went to Raindrop's guesthouse for a few days. She told Branch where she was going, not me. She didn't say anything to me.

I felt bad for what I had done, and at the same time I didn't. I had no desire to hurt Sunny, but she'd betrayed me, kept secrets from me. She did what she wanted to without talking to me about it, so I did the same. I loved Sunny, but I wanted to be with Venus too. The same electric attraction enveloped me with Venus as it did with Sunny. I might even say love blossomed inside me for Venus. Early love, not like I felt for Sunny, but love, nonetheless. Why should I deny myself? I hoped Sunny would realize this could be an exciting new phase of our relationship. Only the beginning, certainly not the end.

I couldn't go over to Raindrop's house. She had made it clear that the only member of Listening Lark welcome there was Sunny. I called and texted Sunny, but she didn't respond. Maybe I should feel guilty, but I didn't. I had decided to do something I felt deeply about, as she did. I don't think being with Venus was a mistake. The universe brought her here for a reason. She was meant to be with me and Sunny. I only had to convince Sunny. She'd forgive me, I was sure.

Two days later I was sick with worry. My earlier bravado dissipated. What was I thinking? Sunny would never forgive me. The sunshine of my life now gone forever. The best thing in my life, ever. I loved her and I betrayed her. I was such a jerk. A stupid jerk. I wanted to go over to Raindrop's house to see her so badly. I called River to see if he thought this was a good idea. He didn't. He told me Sunny was very upset and it probably was a good idea to give her some time. I didn't take his advice.

Last night I went over to Raindrop's house. It was strange being back there even though not much time had passed since I moved out. Even stranger was the quietness. Nobody lounged by the pool; only a lone lime-green raft floated atop the crystal blue water. The kitchen light blazed inside the house when I walked past, but I was only interested in the dim lamp lit inside the pool house.

And the woman inside.

My woman.

I hesitated at the door, debating knocking or just walking inside. I chose to knock. Sunny opened the door. Her hair was in a high ponytail, and she wore a pink pajama set.

She looked gorgeous. How could I have fucked up so badly?

Her eyes narrowed. "I told you not to come here."

She slammed the door shut. A key turned.

Locked out.

Locked out of her heart.

I took a deep breath. *Calmness and balance. Calmness and balance.* I repeated the words in my mind.

"Sunny, please open the door," I called.

"Go away, Dream!" she yelled from inside. "I don't want to talk to you!"

Anger flared inside of me. A brief flicker. "Let's just talk. I was wrong," I said; an edge had crept into my voice. "But you were too."

"I didn't cheat on you! And you hurt me! How could you?" Sunny screamed behind the door. "Get out of here. I don't want to see you!"

My body tensed. The flickers of anger grew stronger inside me. So familiar. Like last time.

"Let me in!" I screamed, banging on the door. "Let me in the damn door!"

Silence from the other side. Nothing, which further infuriated me. Didn't she care about us? About me? Why couldn't she even talk to me?

I kicked the door, over and over again, and continued to pound on it. "If you don't open this door, I'll break it down! We have to talk!"

Strong hands pulled me back, away from the door.

"Stop it, Dream," River yelled at me. "Go back to your house. This isn't helping."

I was sweating now and felt dizzy from all the emotions swirling inside me. I looked at River, his jaw set firmly, his words stern. What was I doing? This type of behavior would not win Sunny back.

I went back to Grandmother's house.

When I got back home, I tossed and turned in my bed most of the night, alone. I had told Venus yesterday I needed some time alone. I hadn't thought all of this through. I hadn't thought at all. If Sunny didn't forgive me, what would I do? How could I earn her trust back? I still held a slight hope she would come back to me. Maybe me and Venus. After all I am a dreamer.

No, that was only a dream. She never would. Would she?

She texted me four days later.

Pick me up tomorrow at 11:00. We'll go to the mountains to talk. I'll bring a picnic lunch. Bring Venus too.

Oh, wow. She wanted to talk to Venus, too? I typed.

Are you sure? Maybe we should talk alone first?

Three dots.

If this is going to work, we need to communicate. All three of us.

Relief flooded me. Oh, it was happening, really happening. This was really going to work out for me. For us. All of us.

FIFTY-THREE
2017

The Commune
Sunny

I can't say I was surprised when I walked in on Dream and Venus. Shocked, yes, but not surprised. The moment I knew he was attracted to her, I felt the shift. He wanted both of us. Dream always got what he wanted.

He was so furious with me about the fiasco with Raindrop. I understood that leaving the guesthouse was a disappointment. I loved it there too, but it wasn't ours. It wasn't like we were homeless; we had a nice home at his grandmother's house. And calling the cops? He never told me anything specific about his past, nor did I, so how should I know I put him at risk by calling them? I was only trying to help Raindrop. She was my friend.

But I'd never witnessed him so consumed with anger. As if he was a different person, not the loving, carefree dreamer I fell in love with, but a hateful, vengeful man I didn't recognize.

Except I did recognize this type of man.

But I would never have imagined Dream fit into that category.

I was so thankful for my friendship with Raindrop. She let me move back into the guesthouse for as long as I liked. It was different living there without Dream, without the other family members. And Raindrop and River were so happy together. I was happy for both of them.

Dream wasn't the first man to break my heart. No, that honor went to my father. He was a man who had held odd parallel values; on one hand he valued the importance of me being able to defend myself. He took me with him target shooting every Sunday afternoon. He was a cop and needed to keep his skill sharp. I started going with him at age thirteen, and in a couple years my shooting skills outshone his, much to his delight.

On the other hand, he was an abusive SOB toward my timid mother. She used to be a secretary at the police station and that's how they met, then she quickly became pregnant with me. Don't you love how people say "She got pregnant" as if she did it herself? What a ridiculous phrase. This was a line I heard repeatedly from my father that "She got pregnant" and trapped him. Then he'd punch her in the face, the side, or slip his hands around her neck and squeeze.

I would never be with someone like my father.

Dream wasn't like my father, was he?

Or was I as passive as my mother and ignored what I didn't want to see?

I would not be like my mother, either.

Dream pulled the van into Raindrop's driveway right on time. Venus sat in the passenger side. I walked over to the van, picnic basket in hand, and she jumped out and moved to the backseat. Well, at least we had a hierarchy.

I settled into the seat and met Dream's gaze. I had lost

myself in those dark eyes so many times. His long, thick hair was wild today. Bed head. I knew what that meant.

"Hi, Dream," I said in a neutral tone.

"Hi, Sunny." He smiled, and moved to kiss me. I turned away.

"Let's have our conversation first," I replied.

I turned to look at Venus in the back seat. She was wearing a pink tank top and khaki shorts with hiking sandals, similar to my current outfit. "Hi, Venus."

"Hi, Sunny," she said in a quiet voice.

Her warm brown eyes studied me. Jealousy aside, I could see what Dream saw in her. She was lovely. And by the look in her eyes, I sensed she wanted my approval. She wanted the same as Dream.

A throuple.

This would be an interesting day.

We drove the short distance to the entrance to the hiking path we normally took. The sun hung high, but a pleasant breeze broke the heat of the late morning. We hiked in mostly silence, the only talk being a mention of the weather or the yellow wildflowers that bloomed along the rocks in one area that received abundant sun. Finally, we reached the vista where we'd often held our morning chanting. It was in an isolated area that saw few visitors. We were the only ones there.

Dream carried the picnic basket and blanket. He placed both on a flat grassy spot close to the drop off, affording us a fantastic view, and far enough away from the edge for me. I don't care for heights.

"This is beautiful," remarked Venus, looking around.

"Oh yeah, I forgot this is your first time here. We haven't had any family events here since you joined us." Dream smiled. "Hell of a view."

I nodded. "Why don't you two check out the view and I'll bring over some wine for us to enjoy together."

Dream's eyes lit up. "Thank you, Sunny. That sounds wonderful."

Venus smiled as Dream took her hand and the two of them walked to the edge of the vista, looking into the vast canyon below. What a lovely couple.

I reached into the brown wicker picnic basket, under the red and white checked towel. A bottle of wine lay inside, but that's not what I sought.

I stared at them, remembering the early times with Dream. I loved his freedom, his passion, his ability to live in the moment without hesitation. I thought he was the one to make me whole. The one person who filled the darkness swirling inside of me for so many years. He was different.

But I was wrong.

He wasn't different.

He was the same.

I lifted my tank top and looked at my abdomen. Faded bruises still visible. Not the splotched, purple reddish hue as when Dream gave them to me the day we moved back to Grandmother's house. I'd seen flashes of his anger before, but nothing like this.

My gaze went to Venus again. I was jealous of her, sure. She was beautiful and now she had my Dream, except Dream had changed in a way I could not accept. Maybe he hadn't changed. I supposed he was always that way, but now I really saw him. I would save myself and Venus, because it was only a matter of time until he showed his true self to her, too. That's why I invited her today: It was my duty to warn her.

My hand shook as I drew the 9MM from beneath the towel inside the basket. I steadied and cocked it, took a sigh, and walked toward Dream and Venus, stopping a good distance from them.

"Dream," I said.

He turned, his long hair caught in the wind. His smile slowly disappeared when he saw the gun pointed at him.

"Sunny, what are you doing?" He took a step toward me.

"Stop," I commanded.

He stopped, dropped Venus's hand, and held his hands up. "Okay, why are you doing this?"

"I thought you were so different," I said.

"You're going to shoot me because I disappointed you?" Dream asked. "Put the gun down and just talk to me."

"Yes, Sunny, please put the gun down," Venus said, visibly shaken.

I glanced at her. She seemed so young and naïve even though I was only two years older than her. "This isn't about you, Venus. It's about him. But I do have a reason for inviting you."

"What do you want to say?" he asked. "I thought we were here to work things out."

I lifted my shirt, exposing my bruised abdomen. "What about this? Do you want to talk about this?"

Venus gasped.

"That's right, Venus," I said. "This is what happens when Dream gets mad at you."

Dream shook his head. "That was... an accident. I didn't mean to hurt you."

"Tell me why you're so worried about the cops. Tell me why you did this to me. Tell me why you think it's okay to treat me like this!"

Dream's face softened. "No, no, it's not okay. You're right, I treated you badly, but I can change. I can be different. I'll be the man you want me to be! I'm sorry, Sunny. You're all I want."

Venus shot him a look.

"I mean, it was so dumb. An armed robbery in a convenience store. Stupid, I should have told you about it. I was embarrassed," he continued.

"Really, a robbery?" I paused. "Raindrop told me why you're so worried about the police. Jim Bob told her when they were together."

A silence fell between the three of us. A silence of secrets, lies, and truths.

Dream glared at me, his eyes narrowed. His voice deepened when he spoke. "I doubt that. If that was true, you'd have already pulled the trigger."

He charged toward me.

I squeezed.

The sound of the gunshot was all-consuming, and in the silence that followed I watched Dream fall back and topple over the edge of the cliff. In an instant, he was gone.

"What did you do?" Venus shrieked. Peering over the edge, frantically searching for him. "I don't see him. He's gone!"

My arms had gone limp. I dropped the gun onto the ground and walked over to Venus, standing beside her and repeated her words. "He's gone."

Venus turned to me, tears streaming down her face. "Why did you do that? Why did you shoot him?"

"I didn't want to," I said, staring at the rocks below. "I didn't want to hurt him. I just wanted him to tell me the truth. To tell you the truth. He deceived both of us."

"You had a gun!" she screamed.

"I wanted to show you he's not what he seems. You saw my bruises; you know he cheated on me with *you*! He was the one who made promises to me and broke them. He pretended he was different, but he's not. I was trying to help you. To tell you who he really is!" My voice cracked. "But I never intended to kill him. I only wanted to scare him."

She pushed me away from her and I tripped over a rock, falling onto the dusty ground.

"You killed him! You killed him!" Venus was hysterical now. She jumped on top of me. "Why?"

"Get off of me!" I yelled, pushing her away.

She grabbed my hair and we rolled on the ground. For a second I had her pinned. She grabbed onto the heart locket I wore, the necklace Dream gave me for Christmas. My neck wrenched agonizingly but I reached for Venus's hand just as the clasp broke. She gripped the necklace in her hand. I pushed her harder and she jumped up, but underestimated the edge of the cliff. I watched her topple back, arms flailing, as she fell into the vast canyon, joining Dream.

I stood still, listening for movement, calls, anything, but there was nothing other than the normal outdoor sounds. I picked up my gun from the dusty ground and walked back over to the edge to peer over into the deep gorge below. No fear of heights would stop me, not when my adrenaline kicked in. Nothing stopped me.

There was no sign of either one of them. I leaned further, careful to keep my footing steady. Eventually I stepped back from the edge, my body shaking. I walked back to the picnic basket, sat on the blanket, and pulled out the bottle of wine. I grabbed the corkscrew, popped the cork, and lifted it to my lips, drinking the sweet nectar.

They were gone.

I'd never see Dream again.

Tears streamed down my face.

I sat there for two hours, crying and occasionally drinking, and eventually throwing up a few times. I drank almost half of the wine bottle but poured out the rest after becoming sick. I needed to stay sharp.

I walked to the edge of the vista again—funny how when you really have to do something, you can overcome your fears—and stared into the sharp drop ending in a vast, deep canyon below. The sun was high in the sky now, its heat beating down on me. I listened intently, but all I heard was the chirping of a few birds. I tried not to think of their bodies lying somewhere in the deep recesses of the canyon. The result of my actions. They were gone now. The thing was I hadn't wanted either of them to die. I'd had good intentions. I only wanted to show Venus who Dream really was and to scare him. To scare him into what... being a decent person? I never should have invited Venus here. She was just a fly caught in Dream's web, like me. She didn't deserve to die.

I turned, grabbed the picnic basket and blanket, then headed back to the van. I passed a couple on the way back through the woods, the only people I'd seen all day. I smiled and nodded calmly, and they reciprocated.

I opened the van door, lifted the floor mat, and retrieved the keys. Dream hated carrying keys; he always put them under the mat. I put the picnic basket in the passenger seat. A few minutes later I pulled out of the parking lot and drove to the bus station. I parked the van in a back lot, put the keys back under the floor mat, and grabbed the picnic basket. I removed the purse I'd put in there, a loan from Raindrop, and put the handgun into the leather bag. Then I disposed of the rest of the basket in a dumpster located at the back of the bus station.

I slung the purse over my shoulder, handgun inside, and walked to a café close to the bus station. I sat there for an hour or so, nursing a coffee and a slice of chocolate cake, although I only took one bite. Sugar be damned. I had just killed the love of my life. Maybe I was the poison, not the sugar.

I called an Uber and stopped first at Dream's grandmother's house, the first home we shared together. Branch was cutting vegetables at the kitchen counter when I arrived. I tried to walk past without being noticed, but it didn't work.

"Oh, hey, Sunny." Branch stopped cutting.

"Hi, Branch," I said.

"Is Dream with you?"

I shook my head. "No... uh actually we broke up."

"What?" Branch walked over to me. "Really?"

"We don't want the same things anymore," I sighed. "I'm going to get some of my stuff and stay at Raindrop's a few more days."

He nodded. "You're not leaving Listening Lark, are you?"

"No, I just need some time to myself."

"Where are Dream and Venus?"

"They took the van, said they were going to the beach," I replied.

Branch nodded and touched my arm. "I'm sorry. I hope you come back soon."

"Thanks." I went upstairs, packed my things, threw in one of Dream's T-shirts and returned to the Uber, still waiting for me, to go back to Raindrop's house.

I walked into the guesthouse, eerily silent now, and fell onto the bed, my body shaking, tears flooding, as my emotions exploded over what I had done.

I stayed in the guesthouse for two days, never leaving it. Raindrop stopped in to check on me and I told her I broke up with Dream and he was now with Venus. I also told her I couldn't stay here anymore. She was sympathetic and said there would always be a place for me here. I was grateful for her friendship.

The next day I booked a flight to Philadelphia, using a credit card Aunt Lou had given me for emergencies. I hugged Raindrop goodbye but didn't tell her where I was going. She didn't know where I was from originally. We hadn't talked about our past.

We lived in the here and now.

FIFTY-FOUR

2024

Aimee

Two weeks passed, but no strange surprises. I admit, I was a bit disappointed. In the beginning, I had thought it might be Brother Jim, but as the gifts became more personal, my hopes that Dream may still be alive flourished. It seemed impossible, but who else would know about the dates, the snow people, the gold locket? I still held on to hope, although the longer he took without revealing himself, the more I wondered if it wasn't a reunion he was after. He probably wanted to hurt me. I did shoot him off a cliff.

But what if he had lived?

Even if he'd survived the gunshot, what about the fall into the canyon? I decided not to think about it and to simply be thankful for a quiet life with Archie, my sexy, responsible, and loyal husband. A man I could count on being there for me. A man that I could trust. I couldn't trust Dream; he was just like my father. So, why did I have this intense longing for him? To see him again, to be with him again, to be in love with him again?

I needed help.

Archie had been acting odd since John's shooting, but he would move on eventually. I looked forward to spring, only a few months away, when we could start fresh in this increasingly strange town. I considered Archie's words seriously about not being sure if he wanted to live in Poplin. Maybe we would move on, we could live anywhere, as long as we were together. That was all I cared about.

I stepped out of the shower and dried off with a plush towel, moisturized, and rubbed a leave-in conditioner into my hair. I slathered on lip balm and reached for my robe, hanging on a hook on the back of the bathroom door. I tied the robe tightly around my body, noticing something in the left pocket. I slipped my hand inside and pulled out the object.

A key.

The guesthouse key.

I stared at it. I had worn the robe last night and the key was not there, I'd swear it. Someone put it there within the last twenty-four hours.

I flung open the bathroom door and yelled, "Dream, are you here?"

I listened but all I could hear was the dripping faucet in the bathroom. I closed my eyes and imagined Dream's voice in my head. I wished he was here, but he wasn't. The house remained silent.

Where are you?
And what do you want?

I poured a second cup of coffee and ate a banana while staring at the key now lying on the kitchen island. Archie would be at school until four. If I didn't stop, I'd be staring at this key all day. I didn't even check the house. If Dream wanted to hurt me, he would have done so by now. No, he wanted something else.

Maybe my sanity?

I picked up the key and put it inside my sweater pocket. I walked over to the pantry, got out some cleaning supplies, and headed up to the attic. I had planned to clean the attic today, so that's what I would do. With all the drawing I'd been doing I thought it would make a nice art studio for me. I could set up an easel up there and do larger pencil drawings; and I'd like to give painting a try too. But, first, a good cleaning was required for the dusty attic.

I opened the door at the top of the attic stairs and pulled the string light. The dim light illuminated the room. We would need more light in here if I wanted to use this space. Maybe add a few floor lamps and a comfortable chair by the window. A ceiling fan wasn't a bad idea; the air was stale up here. Also, a heater, maybe one of those electric fireplaces to warm the space.

Sunlight filtered through the pretty stained-glass window at the front of the house and the spider web window, with actual spider webs on it that I needed to wipe, at the back of the house. I grabbed my dust rag and spray. I cleaned away as much dust as possible.

I wiped Archie's file cabinets and pushed them into the corner of the room. Then I moved over to the large mahogany wardrobe, wiping the dust on every corner of the large piece of furniture. This might be a good place to store art supplies. I opened the door, surveying the space. Yes, this would work. I wiped the back, sides, and bottom shelf.

As I wiped the bottom shelf, my rag got stuck on a nub toward the back. I lifted the rag and peered into the wardrobe. All the way in the back was a small, almost flat black button. I pressed it.

The shelf slid open to reveal a hidden compartment below it, filled with items. I stared, recognizing some of the objects. Dream's T-shirt, a few photos from Listening Lark, the dried lotus flowers. Things from the box in my closet.

The attic suddenly felt very quiet. Too quiet. The lurking silence contained a wisp of fear.

I turned around to look behind me.

There was nothing there. My gaze traveled around the attic, but nothing stood out as unusual. I walked over to the attic steps, went down them and closed the door to the stairwell. I didn't want to be disturbed while looking through these items. I had about an hour until Archie got home from school.

I hurried back upstairs and started to sort through the secret shelf. In addition to the things I had already viewed, there was a bag of medjool dates. Also a stack of seven books. No, journals, very familiar journals, especially the leather-bound one from 2017. The journal I gave Dream for Christmas.

My heart leapt.

He was alive. It had been Dream this entire time. He was *alive*!

Would he forgive me?

Would I forgive him?

Would we be together again?

My hands trembled as I opened the journal and read the last entry. The day he and Venus were going on a picnic with me.

The day I killed him.

Or so I thought.

I took a deep breath. I wanted Dream to be here right now, wrapping his arms around me. I would always love him. My love for Archie would never compare to what I still felt for Dream. My hands were still shaking. Was he watching me now?

"Please, Dream, if you are here, let me see you," I pleaded. "Please forgive me. I love you."

Silence was my only answer.

I sighed, wanting so badly for him to be here, to be alive, to forgive me.

I continued to search the contents under the shelf. I pushed the journals and other items to the side. Then, I opened a large manilla envelope. I released its contents onto the floor and sorted through the various pieces. Old family photos. Most of the contents of the envelope were photos. I lifted a stack and something hard fell out.

A driver's license.

I picked it up, staring at the face I knew well.

Archie.

The license had expired a few years ago. I read the address under his name and sank to the floor.

Clear Lake, California.

Archie was from California?

My mind spun in so many directions. What did this mean?

I picked up the photos again. Family pictures. A mother, father, and three children, two boys and a girl, at the beach, standing by a Christmas tree, at a summer picnic. I studied the boys' faces and it was easy to see that Archie was the middle child, with an older brother and a younger sister.

He'd told me his father died from cancer when he was a child, and his sister and mother were killed in a car accident. Who was the other boy? I looked at him again. I didn't know the boy. Why would Archie hide these from me?

My gaze went to the sister, obviously a few years younger than Archie. I flipped through a few more pictures as the children got older.

One photo stunned me.

I could barely breathe.

It couldn't be her.

I stared at the girl, probably around ten years old, standing with Archie, maybe fourteen, and the other boy, probably seventeen or eighteen. They were posing in a yard, wearing shorts and T-shirts. The girl had long dark hair and warm brown eyes. She smiled shyly into the camera.

I knew her.

Venus.

I sat on the floor staring at the photos. I'd been sitting there for what seemed like an eternity, yet likely only ten minutes had passed. Dream was not alive. Venus was not alive. Archie was Venus's brother and was trying to... I didn't know, make me go insane? Why the hell would he marry me? What was his plan?

I went back to the secret compartment. There was a burner phone lying by the journals. I picked it up and swiped. No passcode needed, thank goodness. Recent calls were all to a number in Hillsboro, Oregon. I looked at the texts. All to the same Oregon number.

His friend Nick lived in Oregon.

I had never seen Nick. Maybe he was the boy in the pictures.

Nick was Archie and Venus's brother?

I was getting a headache.

I read through the texts. Mostly about bank deposits and transfers. Some references about "her," obviously me, stating how I had no clue and how I deserved to be broke after what I did. Other derogatory statements that I ignored. I was mad enough already. I focused on the bank transfers. Archie had been sending Nick, if that was his real name, a lot of money. My money.

That's the reason he married me.

But why seek me out after so many years? How would he know what I did to Venus? How did he have Dream's journals?

I picked up another photo and flipped it around. In neat handwriting, *Nick, 17, Archie, 14, Caroline, 11*. So Venus's real name was Caroline. And Nick was definitely their brother. I looked at one other item in the secret hiding space, a Wi-Fi enabled light with a remote control. I groaned. That must be the light I saw in the attic over the summer when I was home alone. Archie could control it from school. What a sneaky jerk. I put everything back exactly as I found it and closed the secret compartment. Archie would be home soon.

My feelings swirled in so many directions inside me. I'd have thought I would feel hurt that my husband betrayed me and tricked me into falling for him and believing his feelings were real, but my overriding emotion was anger, mixed with hurt yes, but anger seeped through every part of my body.

One plus: I didn't have anything to fear. Now it was the others, Archie and Nick, who should be very afraid. They assumed they knew things about me, but now they would know first-hand.

FIFTY-FIVE

2018

Archie

I hadn't heard from Caroline in almost a year. After not answering my repeated calls and texts for months, and going to the apartment she rented in LA with another girl who taught yoga in the same studio, I was at a dead end. The roommate, Grace, wasn't much help. Caroline had only lived with her for two months. She said some older guy with long hair had picked Caroline up when she'd told Grace she was moving out. Grace was mad because Caroline still owed rent—which I gave her—and Caroline said she was going somewhere she could live rent free and that she *lived in the here and now*. The roommate remembered that exact phrase because it sounded so weird to her.

None of the story sat well with me, or our older brother, Nick. Caroline was in trouble and the sooner we found her, the better. I wrote down the phrase the roommate mentioned and did an internet search on it, but nothing popped up that led anywhere. I had to find my sister.

The search was at a dead end until a strange thing

happened one day. I was visiting a friend in Santa Monica, and we went to a farmers' market. As we were looking at fresh peaches at a stand, I overheard someone say that phrase, "we live in the here and now."

I turned to see a stand behind me filled with fresh fruits and vegetables, bottles of wine, and beautiful turquoise jewelry. A man with long blond hair, up in a bun, stood in the center, giving change to an elderly woman purchasing a necklace. A beautiful woman with long raven hair, dressed in a flowing white gown with gold embroidery, spoke to a young man, probably in his late teens. She was the one speaking.

"Excuse me," I interrupted her. "What did you just say about the here and now?"

She smiled and repeated the phrase.

I was so excited, and my story spilled out of me about my sister. The woman, Moonbeam, was very kind and directed me to the man with the man bun, Branch. I showed him a picture of Caroline on my phone, and he told me she was now called Venus. He also told me the story about Dream, Venus, and Sunny.

Dream and Venus never returned from a picnic Sunny planned, and soon after, Sunny disappeared.

Branch told me to stop by Listening Lark. All of Dream's and Venus's personal items were boxed in the basement. I was welcome to look through it if I wished.

Today I stood in the damp, tiny basement of the commune called Listening Lark. I appreciated Branch and Moonbeam's cooperation, but what the hell did Caroline get herself into? She joined a commune and, according to Branch, was involved in a relationship with a couple?

I sorted through the plastic container holding her clothes, makeup, jewelry. Not that much, really. She had a journal, so that may turn out to be helpful. I looked through Dream's plastic bin. How was a grown-ass man called Dream? All these new names were insane. Caroline being called Venus? I wondered if she was drugged the whole time she was here. Everything about this was crazy to me.

Emotions filled me as I looked through the meager items left of my baby sister's life. I knew she would be in contact with me if she could. I knew she must be gone, but she deserved so much more than this. She was bright, smart, and funny. I loved her, and I missed her so much. This group and these people just used her and threw her away like trash. Tears welled in my eyes.

And I hadn't protected her.

Dream's container held mostly clothes, some books, and six journals. I took all his journals. It looked like he wrote in them every day for three years. Hopefully, the entries would give some insight to what happened to them. I opened one and a couple photos fell out.

I picked them off the floor. A tall guy with long, dark hair with his arm around a pretty petite blonde girl. They stood by a pool wearing bathing suits. The girl was very tan and gorgeous. Was this Sunny? I flipped the photo over: *Dream and Sunny, 2016.*

I wished Sunny would have left something behind. From what Branch said, she left in a hurry after the picnic lunch with Dream and my sister. Branch said Sunny walked in on the two of them in bed and Dream was pushing for a relationship with both of them. Who was this guy? This asshole that ruined my sister's life.

I'd start with the journals. I took Caroline's container, including Dream's journals and photos, and walked upstairs.

FIFTY-SIX

2021

Archie

After reading all the journals, I had Sunny's real first and last name, and knew that she'd lived in Philadelphia with her aunt Lou in Society Hill. Dream documented all of this on the first day he met her. I guessed this was before she lived in the here and now.

There was so little about my sister in Dream's journal and so much about Sunny. He lusted after Caroline, aka Venus, but he loved Sunny. Caroline's journal was scant and other than showing she had a crush on Dream, was basically useless. I was certain finding Sunny would give me answers I wanted to find, but I'd have to get close to her first.

What would I do after I found out the truth? I was certain Sunny had something to do with Dream's and Caroline's disappearance. Did she kill them? I was sure of it. Caroline would have contacted me, even if she'd run off with that guy.

Would I kill Sunny?

I didn't know.

I wanted justice for my sister. She was my family; I was

supposed to keep her safe. It made me sick thinking of what might have happened to her. She deserved so much better. Nick felt the same, but he wasn't obsessed with it like me; even so, it took me years to make the move to Pennsylvania. It was a big move and I wasn't even sure what I would do when I arrived, but I made the decision to move, and find Sunny, or Aimee, or whatever the hell name she went by now.

I moved into my new apartment in January, not too far from Society Hill; I couldn't afford anything in that neighborhood, and was lucky to find a teaching job midway through the school year. There were two elderly women that might fit for Aimee's aunt Lou: Louann Bixler and Louise Atwater. When I wasn't at school, I was watching these homes, hoping to catch a glimpse of Aimee at one of them. For the first three months, there was nothing.

Finally, I saw her come out of Louise Atwater's house. I recognized her instantly, and was shocked at how beautiful I found her in person. Now I knew where she lived. I followed her to an organic grocery store where she bought a few items and then went home. Then, after a month of watching her, she walked to a nearby coffee shop. She was in line and put in her order, but also asked to speak to the manager about a job. I was going to approach her then, but hung back; if she did get a job here, it would be so much easier to meet her.

A week later, I walked into the coffee shop to pick up an order for school. Aimee was working. I asked her out that day. And my plan was set into motion.

We dated, but I wasn't sure what I was doing. I was attracted to her, but I didn't trust her. I had only wanted to be friends with her and get close to her in that way, at least that had been my plan, but we had an undeniable attraction for each other.

One day, I was sitting at my desk at school waiting for the

magic hour of four o'clock so I could leave. My cell phone rang. Aimee.

"Hello?"

She was crying on the other end.

"What's wrong?" I asked.

"Aunt Lou died. She fell down the stairs."

"Oh no, I'm sorry," I said. "I'm on my way."

I hurried to the hospital and took Aimee into my arms as she cried. I smoothed back her hair. "I'm sorry. Is there someone I should call for you?"

She shook her head. "No, I'm Aunt Lou's only relative. Her only heir."

"Oh." I hugged her again, and a plan formulated in my mind. Aunt Lou was loaded. I wouldn't kill Aimee, I couldn't do that, but I would take her money. Not that it would make up for what she'd done to Caroline, but it would help.

I knew Aimee killed my sister.

I think she killed her aunt Lou too.

FIFTY-SEVEN

2024

Archie

I sat in the school parking lot staring at my phone. After my conversation with Nick, I knew everything was over. She'd held him at gunpoint until he transferred all the balances back to her, in an account with her name only. Aimee knew what we were up to; she knew we were Caroline's brothers, or as she knew her, Venus. I hadn't really thought out my plan with Aimee and guilt flooded me knowing I'd put my brother and this small town in danger by bringing a murderer here. I didn't count on my plan of stealing her money to put other people in danger of being killed. People I truly liked and thought of as my friends. By now, I was in too deep, and I didn't know how to get out, other than to complete what I started and get the hell away from Aimee. I was thankful she hadn't killed Nick. Surprised, too.

I didn't want to move to Poplin. I didn't want to live on a farm and have chickens and raise vegetables, but Aimee did. I needed several months to make the bank transfers discreetly and without her noticing, so whatever she wanted to do, we did.

Dream's journals were invaluable with the information they

contained about Aimee. While they didn't help me find out what happened to Caroline, they did give me an intimate look into Aimee's likes, her time spent in Listening Lark, and the relationship she had had with Dream.

I started with leaving the dates that Dream mentioned several times in the journal as her favorite. I ordered a couple bags online and kept them in the wardrobe along with everything else inside the hidden drawer. It was easy finding the other items she kept in a shoebox in her closet, marked LL on the front.

I wanted to scare her a bit, and keep her on edge, unsure of who was sending these items. Anything to distract her from the bank accounts that I was slowly draining every day. Eventually when I divorced her, I hoped within a year, I'd have most of her money. I opened a home equity loan on the farm to drain that asset too. She'd be lucky to be able to live in one of those cabins she occupied with Dream at Listening Lark by the time I was done.

I found it funny how she never told me about anything, except the light on in the attic. I knew she would be picking green beans while I was away, so I set up the wireless light in the attic. She was so freaked out. I laughed so hard when she texted me about it. I enjoyed playing mind games with her. It wasn't close to what I'm certain she did to Caroline and Dream. If I was a different person, the payback would be much more permanent.

When Angela was murdered, I wondered for a moment if Aimee was involved. Had she found the note in my pocket? Angela had flirted with me, and she wasn't subtle. If Aimee found that note, it may have triggered something in her. I dismissed the thought because it seemed too much even for her.

But then Robin. There was no way she'd died by accident. She was so attentive to her allergy and careful about always having an EpiPen close by. An allergy attack wouldn't have taken her down so fast that she couldn't have reached the EpiPen in the drawer so close to her. Aimee had to be involved. I wondered if she saw Robin and I in the grocery store parking lot when Robin kissed me. Was she grocery shopping, or following me, if she saw us? I pulled away from Robin not because I didn't want to kiss her. I did want to, very much so in fact, but I knew Aimee would destroy her. And she did. Robin and I were great friends and maybe in a year or two, when I was divorced, we could have been more than friends. The feelings were there, but the time wasn't right. Little did I know I'd never get that chance. Her death was such a surprise to me. Aimee and Robin were friends and Aimee seemed to genuinely like her. She must have witnessed that single kiss in the parking lot and decided that was it for Robin. Would she have killed me too if I returned the kiss?

As time went on, I realized how dangerous Aimee was—more so than I originally thought. I had married a serial killer. I should have stayed in California, but it was too late for regrets now. I'd gotten myself into a real mess with a psychopath and one question remained. *How do I get away from her?*

Now she knew everything. And I knew she wouldn't grant me the same leniency as she gave my brother.

There was only one way for me to get out alive.

Kill her.

FIFTY-EIGHT

2024

Aimee

A week had passed since I'd found out the truth about Archie. I arrived home today after four days away. I'd told Archie I needed to go finalize some things with Aunt Lou's estate. Funny how he was so agreeable whenever I mentioned anything with her estate. He brightened up like a light bulb. More money for him and his brother.

Or so he thought...

I unpacked my suitcase and put on jeans and a soft, loose sweatshirt. I glanced at the clock. Archie would be home soon. The house was filled with savory smells of the roast beef in the oven. In a minute I'd set up our dinner in the dining room but now I stared at my reflection in the vanity mirror. Still young, still pretty, I supposed, but tired. Tired of everything life continued to throw at me. I smiled at myself in the mirror. I knew one thing though.

I was a survivor.

The candles flickered, their movement casting dancing

shadows on the pale painted walls. Dinner was set for two atop a white lacy tablecloth. Etched glass goblets filled with water and red wine stood tall at each dinner place. Fancy, for a weeknight.

I sat at one end of the table in the dining room, facing the kitchen. I had been watching by the living room window for Archie's arrival and quickly placed the food on the table. A moist roast beef swimming in rich juices with a few sprigs of bright green parsley at the side, mashed potatoes with butter melting, a bowl of precisely diced carrots, and a basket of freshly baked buttermilk biscuits. A meal fit for a king.

Maybe his last meal.

The door opened in the laundry room at the rear of the house and, a few minutes later, Archie appeared in the doorway, his hair tousled, dressed in a smart-looking forest green dress shirt. I forgot for a moment about everything going on and stared at him. He was so good looking. So kind. So supportive. He was my miracle after what went down with Dream. A man I could trust. A man that would always be there for me.

But he wasn't.

He was playing games.

Like they all did.

I smiled and motioned for him to sit down, and he acquiesced. He sat stiffly, his body barely touching the back of the chair.

We stared at each other.

For a long time.

Archie cleared his throat. "When did you get back?"

"This afternoon," I said. "I had plenty of time to cook dinner."

He nodded. "I see that, everything looks great."

"Help yourself," I said, taking a sip of wine; a bit dripped down my chin. I wiped it away with my napkin, my gaze never leaving Archie.

He stared at the food with a disgusted look on his face. Did he think I'd poisoned the food?

Maybe I had.

"So you know everything now," he mumbled. His gaze never wavered from mine.

"I do," I said. "I saw your brother, Nick, today."

"I know, he called me." Archie pushed back in his chair, letting out a deep sigh.

"You can thank me for that," I quipped, raising my eyebrows.

"What?" Archie snapped.

"You can thank me that your brother is still alive," I said in a terse voice. "I could have left him in a different state."

He gave me a seething look. "But you killed Caroline."

I met his gaze. "Not intentionally."

Archie jumped up and pounded his fist on the table, causing his goblets to fall over; red wine spilled onto the winter white tablecloth. "You killed my sister!" His eyes blazed with anger.

I stood and met his gaze. "Venus fell over the cliff because she was fighting with me over Dream. I didn't want to kill him either, but he came after me! I only wanted to scare him and show your sister his true colors. But she couldn't see how I was helping her. Just like my mother."

Archie's body slightly relaxed, his eyes now holding more curiosity than anger. "What do you mean?"

I looked away for a moment, wondering if he really did care, and what that might mean to me. To us.

"Aimee, tell me."

I looked back to him. Unexpected emotions flooded through me. He did care about me, in spite of everything. My breathing slowed. Maybe we could work through this and still be a couple? We'd both hurt each other; could we manage to forgive?

Move away, maybe a city this time. I didn't think the country was for us.

"Aimee," he repeated, impatient.

I stared at him. I took a breath. I would try.

"My dad was abusive toward my mom. He would hit her, say vile things to her, all in front of me. It's what I remember most about my childhood." I paused. Tears threatened to spill, but I willed them away. "That, and the day I killed him."

Archie's eyes widened. He kept his distance, but his voice softened. "You killed your father?"

I nodded. "Mom and I came home from shopping and found him half naked with the neighbor lady. After the lady ran away, Dad threw Mom against the wall, choking her so hard." I stopped, my hands shaking.

"I'm sorry, Aimee," Archie said, hesitant. He almost seemed like he wanted to hug me but held back. "What happened next?"

"I went to the gun cabinet, took out the 9MM I used for target shooting. Dad was a cop and took me target shooting every Sunday," I said flatly. "I shot him. And he died."

"And your mom?"

"Resented me, even though I did it for her, to protect her, until she drove her car onto the train tracks. They said her car stalled, but I know she waited for it. She wanted to die too, to be with him. She blamed me for everything. She'd told me so earlier that day."

"Your mom blamed you?" Archie asked.

I met his gaze. "Just like your sister. I promise, Archie, I didn't want to hurt her."

A mix of emotions flashed across his face until anger settled in. "You lured her there!"

"Yes, I wanted her there. I wanted her to see the truth about Dream. And if she wasn't there and Dream went missing, she'd go right to Brother Jim. I didn't want that happening. She couldn't see that I was doing it for both of us."

"How could she? You're crazy! You say you didn't want to kill my sister, but you did!" He glared at me. "Did you kill Robin too?"

He didn't believe me. He didn't love me. I felt my heart breaking again.

FIFTY-NINE
SEPTEMBER 2023

Aimee

I placed the thermos of vegetable soup into my tote bag and did a quick check of Archie. He was still sleeping on the sofa. He'd be out for a while. I'd added just enough sleeping pills to his cup of tea for a solid nap.

I bundled up and walked the short distance to Robin's farm. It was cold and dark on the lonely country road, but not windy so it wasn't too bad.

I knew I must be as discreet as possible.

The lights were on downstairs, and I saw Robin moving around in the kitchen. I hoped she hadn't eaten dinner yet.

I put a bright, friendly smile on my face and rang her doorbell. I saw her walk toward the door through the sheer curtains on the glass panel on the front door. She opened the door, surprised to see me.

"Aimee!" She smiled. "Come in."

"Hey, I made some vegetable soup and thought you might like some for dinner." I held up the thermos.

"Oh, that's perfect," she said. "I was just wondering what to have."

"Great," I replied, taking off my coat.

"I didn't see your headlights." She poured some of the soup into a bowl. "Usually, they shine in the windows of the house when you go around the turn in the lane."

I nodded, watching her grab a spoon and eat the soup. I made small talk for a few minutes as she ate.

"This is really good soup," she remarked. "Has a bit of a different taste than usual."

I smiled, but didn't respond. That unusual taste was ground peanuts in the soup broth. A few minutes passed until she started gasping. Her face swelled, as I expected.

"Aimee, my EpiPen." She fumbled in her kitchen drawer, then tried to reach her purse on the kitchen counter. I moved it farther away.

Not that it mattered. All her EpiPens were in my tote bag. I took them a few days before when I slept over here. It was amazing how fast it happened. Robin stumbled and fell on the kitchen floor, wheezing.

Then she silenced.

Permanently.

I put on plastic gloves and hurried around the kitchen to complete my mission. I took out a container of vegetable soup from my tote bag that I had purchased from the grocery store, poured about three quarters of it down the sink, then added a bit of my peanut laced soup to it and placed it in the refrigerator. I put my thermos back into my bag. Then, I replaced all the EpiPens that I had taken back into their normal spots.

Mission complete.

I slung my tote bag on my arm, and surveyed the area to make sure everything was as it should be. My gaze went to Robin, now lying dead on her parents' kitchen floor.

It was a shame. I really liked her. We were becoming good

friends, but that was an illusion. She was never really my friend. The only friend she really wanted was Archie. And I wasn't going to let that happen. I had learned from my past.

Three weeks ago, I was at the grocery store when I saw them standing in the parking lot. Archie told me they were going shopping together for some supplies for a science project both classes were doing the following week. They stood by her car, talking, and I almost walked over to join them, but hesitated. They put the grocery bags into her trunk. She closed it, then turned to Archie, moving closer. She leaned in, they were about the same height, he was only slighter taller than her, and kissed him.

On the lips.

He backed away, hesitating a moment, which I didn't like, but he did back away, and shook his head.

They talked for a few more minutes, him standing a substantial distance from her, and each got into their cars and left the parking lot.

Goodbye, Robin.

I turned around and walked out the door.

SIXTY

2024

Aimee

"I killed Robin," I said calmly. "And Angela. I saw Robin kiss you in the parking lot, and I found the love note Angela gave you."

"But why? Why would you do that?" he asked, moving closer to me. He stopped midway across the room.

I rounded the table and stood a few feet away from him. "They were a threat to me. A threat to this beautiful life I created with you. I wouldn't let them take you away from me. I'm supposed to be the center of your world, and I don't share with anyone."

Archie stared at me, his emotions tucked away, unreadable. But the vein on the right side of his neck pulsated, a physical indication of his surging anger. "So, you killed them? And what about Aunt Lou? You killed that sweet old woman for her money!"

Heat crept through my body, my burning inside fury, always present, mounted into an inferno at the disgusting, vile words he spat at me. I would *never* hurt Aunt Lou. Never! I didn't kill her; it was an accident. I loved Aunt Lou.

I lunged at Archie, catching him by surprise, and pushed him down, his face going into the bowl of mashed potatoes. I eyed the serving knife, shiny, sharp steel, lying next to the roast beef platter. Archie jerked up, pushing me onto the floor.

"You killed all of these people!" he screamed. Mashed potatoes smeared across his face. He swiped it with his hand. His eyes gleamed with fury through the white substance.

I jumped up and ran around the table. "I did not kill Aunt Lou! Never say that again."

"You expect me to believe that?" he roared, rounding the table behind me.

"I didn't kill Nick either," I screamed. "And I could have."

"Fucking psycho." Archie snatched the knife from the table

I ran into the kitchen, reached into my back jeans pocket, and retrieved my handgun.

Archie charged me with the knife, but he stopped when I pointed the gun at him.

They always do.

"Oh, now you're going to shoot me? How are you going to get away with that?"

A closet door squeaked open in the laundry room. I'd been expecting it. I had also expected the person waiting in there to join us. It certainly took him long enough. Relief shone in Archie's eyes for a second, until he registered what the man was doing.

John Larabe stood on my side of the kitchen, dressed in his usual blue work shirt and giant belt buckle. He reached behind him and retrieved a handgun, then directed it at Archie.

"Probably self-defense, but I'm going to do it so she doesn't have to worry about it."

John pulled the trigger, and Archie collapsed to the ground.

SIXTY-ONE

2024

Aimee

Archie's death was ruled self-defense. John testified that he had stopped by that evening to see Archie and heard yelling inside the house. He had entered through the unlocked laundry door and saw Archie charging at me with a knife. He discharged his weapon, perfectly legal with his concealed carry permit, to defend me. I corroborated his story and also shared with the police that Archie had admitted to killing Angela. He became enraged when confronted with the note I found in his coat pocket from Angela. I got lucky with that one: The old note was still in the seldom worn coat pocket. He admitted to me that they were having an affair and he'd killed her. Of course, that was only hearsay, but he wasn't around to say anything, so I had an advantage.

Dead.

So many dead.

Because of me.

I didn't feel good about any of it, but I knew that I'd only done what I needed to do. I was a survivor, not only physically, but emotionally, too. I could have killed Archie, but I didn't want to. Yes, he betrayed me, lied to me, and played games with me. He was avenging his sister's death. I could understand that, even respect it. As a whole, he was a good person.

After John's warning in his driveway I knew I had to act fast. The guy was going to destroy me. I needed to dangle something in front of him that he desperately wanted. Unfortunately, I couldn't allow Archie to live, but I could have John do my dirty work.

Then I knew.

He wanted the farm. And that's what he got.

John isn't a good person. Nor am I, but at least I have a logic to my train of thought, an individual moral code. Conventional, perhaps not, but it makes sense to me. Sure, I tried shooting John while he was rabbit hunting. I went hunting all the time with my father and I'm an excellent shot. Who knew he'd be wearing a bulletproof vest though? Not a common practice for hunters.

John's a grabber. He wants things, people, respect, not because he deserves it—he just wants it. He wanted Robin, despite her feelings about him. I could have taken care of Archie on my own, but this story was much more believable. I must give John credit; he saw me. The real me. Makes me wonder about his past, but I'm not that interested. He fulfilled his purpose, and he won't bother me again.

Now that everything was settled with the police, tomorrow I would sign the papers giving the farm to John. A gesture of goodwill for saving my life. At least that's what we're telling people.

I finished packing my dishes and taped the box shut. My phone beeped as a text popped up. I saw who it was from and smiled. Raindrop, well her real name is Emma, sent me her new address in Malibu. I pressed to like the text.

We'd been talking lately and she asked me to come visit her

and River, now Greg; they are both back to their given names. I'm flying out next week. I'll be getting a new identity, thanks to Greg's contacts, because one loose end still exists: Nick. I doubt he will seek me out; I gave him a chance and warned him it would be his last. He has a family and as much as he loved his brother and sister, I don't think he will risk his own personal safety and that of his family to spill the truth on me. But I'm not taking any chances. I will be Charlotte Applewood. This name is special to me, as Charlotte was Aunt Lou's middle name. A new beginning in a familiar place.

Back to California.

I live in the here and now.

EPILOGUE
2011

David

The garage door was open and Kelsey stood inside waving me in. I pulled my car inside, killed the engine, and she hit the automatic garage opener, closing the door behind me.

I got out of the car and she was in my arms, kissing me.

"I don't want the neighbors to be curious about a strange car in the driveway."

I laughed and returned her kisses. I'd met Kelsey in a restaurant two months ago near Berkeley, where I was a sophomore. It was casual hookups at first, but I was developing feelings for her. She was beautiful and funny. We usually hung out at my dorm room, which worked out pretty well because my roommate was usually out. This was my first time at her house. I'd never met any of her family or friends, but in all fairness, she'd only met my roommate once or twice. I felt amazing with Kelsey, like I could accomplish anything. In my mind, I was playing out scenes when her parents came home from work later, how I'd shake her father's hand and he'd call me "son."

Kelsey's hands were all over me, bringing me back from my

daydreams. She laughed, took my hand, and led me into the house, down the hallway to her bedroom.

We tumbled onto her bed, already unmade, throwing our clothes to the floor and fucked like we always did. Frantic, hot, passionate.

We were lying in her bed, sweaty and spent, when her cell rang. She picked it up from the nightstand and glanced at it.

"Oh, I'll call him back later," she said. She put the phone back on the nightstand.

"Who?" I asked, stretching my arms.

"My boyfriend."

I stopped stretching and stared at her. I couldn't understand what I had just heard. "Your boyfriend?"

Kelsey gave me a coy smile. "Yeah, I probably should have told you. He's in college at NYU."

"Really."

"Um... I mean you and I are just casual, right?"

"Sure," I said. Anger raced through me. I felt so stupid. Why had I thought it could be more?

She rolled over to me, rubbing my chest. "I mean, you're kind of..."

"What?"

"You don't want to be in a relationship. You are kind of... flaky."

I sat up. "You think I'm flaky? What does that even mean?"

"Um... I don't know." Kelsey continued to talk, but I barely heard what she said. Heat flooded my body and I just wanted her to shut up. I wasn't good enough for her. I was too *flaky*!

The rejection hurt.

"Shut up! Shut up!" I screamed. Rage consumed me now, filling every fiber in my body. My hands went around Kelsey's slim neck and I squeezed. So hard. Squeezing. Squeezing. I watched as her arms and legs flailed about, trying to escape my grasp.

Then silence.

Calm.

Her lifeless body was limp in my grasp. I let go.

I panicked, pacing around the bedroom, Kelsey's body lying motionless and breathless in her unmade bed.

What the fuck am I going to do?

I just killed somebody.

I sat on the bed and contemplated the situation. If Kelsey was found, I would go to jail for murder.

I could not go to jail.

I knew what I needed to do. I stood and went back to the garage. A pair of work gloves were on the workbench at the side. I put them on and searched through the shelves, looking for something I could put Kelsey's body into. I found an extra-large dark green duffel bag that would work.

I took the bag into the house, stuffed Kelsey's body inside, along with some of her clothing, hoping to make it look like she went on a trip. I stripped the bed, I couldn't leave my DNA here, and tossed them in the bag too. Next I found the linen closet, put fresh sheets on the bed, and finally wiped any surfaces I'd touched with a packet of Clorox wipes found on the kitchen counter.

I grabbed Kelsey's cell phone, typed a quick message to the boyfriend and her mom that she was going on a girls' trip to Vegas, then wiped the phone too. I hauled the duffel bag out to the garage, popped the trunk, put her body inside and slammed it shut.

Had it really only been an hour since I'd first pulled into the garage? How was that possible? Kelsey's phone lit up with two incoming texts.

Have fun! Be safe. I love you.

That was from her mom.

Okay, call me later.

That was from her *boyfriend*.

I sighed, pressed the button to open the garage door and backed out of the driveway.

I drove out of the neighborhood, headed home to Santa Monica. On a lonely stretch of highway, I pulled off to the side of the road, threw Kelsey's phone on the ground and drove over it several times. Finally, leaving it cracked, broken, and dead.

Just as I had done to Kelsey.

I arrived at Grandmother's house shortly after nine p.m. Jim Bob lived here now since Grandmother died a few months ago and left the house to us. I'd called him on my drive and explained the situation.

He said he had a plan.

I wouldn't go to jail.

I thought about what he told me last month. His idea of building the group, the family, he had already started in the Valley. Taking it to another level with Grandmother's house as the headquarters. Listening Lark, he called it. It sounded interesting and especially now after all that had happened. I planned to drop out of Berkeley. I couldn't continue to live there after what happened.

I smelled smoke when I arrived at Grandmother's house. I walked around to the backyard. A large bonfire blazed in the yard. Jim Bob sat in a yellow lawn chair smoking a cigar.

"Hey," I said.

He rose from his chair. "Hey, David, let's get this done."

We went to the car, retrieved the duffel bag containing Kelsey's body and tossed it into the burning flames.

"Thanks for helping me, Jim Bob," I said as I watched the flames.

Jim Bob took a long drag from his cigar, watching me. "Of course, we're family."

"So, this Listening Lark idea, I think I'm interested," I said, trying to hide the anxiety in my voice. "I'm dropping out of college."

He nodded. "Good idea to lay low for a while. We'll give you a new name too. I think I'll give all members a new name since Listening Lark is a new beginning."

I nod. "So what should it be?"

Jim Bob paused for a moment. "How about Dream? You've always been a dreamer."

My laugh sounded hollow to my ears, but I pasted a smile onto my face. "Dream. I like it."

"Oh, and did I tell you our mantra? It's perfect for you."

"What is it?"

Jim Bob grinned. "We live in the here and now."

A LETTER FROM THE AUTHOR

Huge thanks for reading *The Forever Home*; I hope you were hooked by Aimee's dramatic life, both in the present and the past. If you want to join other readers in hearing all about my new releases and bonus content, you can sign up for my newsletter.

www.stormpublishing.co/sally-royer-derr

If you enjoyed this book and could spare a few moments to leave a review that would be hugely appreciated. Even a short review can make all the difference in encouraging a reader to discover my books for the first time. Thank you so much!

The Forever Home started with a few ideas and developed into a complicated, dramatic story that was exciting to write and I hope exciting for you to read. The changes suggested by my editor, Emily Gowers, gave this story even more dramatic impact. I'm so happy to share this book with my readers and look forward to hearing your thoughts about the story.

Thanks again for being part of this amazing journey with me and I hope you'll stay in touch—I have so many more stories and ideas to entertain you with!

Sally

KEEP IN TOUCH WITH THE AUTHOR

www.sallyroyer-derr.com

facebook.com/SallyRoyerDerrAuthorPage

x.com/sallyroyerderr

instagram.com/srderr

bookbub.com/profile/sally-royer-derr

tiktok.com/@sallyroyerderr

ACKNOWLEDGEMENTS

Many thanks to my editor, Emily Gowers. Collaborating with you inspires my creativity and working on this book with you has been a pleasure. Also, thank you to the entire team at Storm Publishing. Your support and thoughtfulness are very much appreciated.

Thanks to Mike, Bradley, and Bella—I love you. Thanks to all my family and friends who have supported my writing throughout the years. Your excitement for my writing journey means so much to me.

A warm thank you to my readers for reading my books and writing wonderful reviews. I am deeply grateful for your support.

Made in the USA
Middletown, DE
06 July 2024